The Man Who Would Have Been

By
J.J. Mortensen

Dedicated to
my darling, Myrkka.
Through the dark angry nights, the silent exploration
of questions, the expert dart games and long, late,
drunken rants, she never once told me to shut up, and
always told me to keep writing.

Thanks to:

My wonderful parents, John and Jan Mortensen,
Who taught me the value of literature and ensured the lessons
interred within lived on.

My dear brother Christopher Mortensen,
The man who shared a childhood of books and the results which
followed us.

My friend Javier Lopez, the exact opposite of the
portrait I paint,
One of the kindest souls I've ever known.

Jessica Levake,
Whose gift of a beautiful notebook resulted in this, and many
more ideas, I can never thank her enough.

My dear friends and fellow writers,
Grant Dempsey, Sandip Roy, and Mark Beachem
whose faith and support never wavered.

My high school English teachers, Deanna Malvesti and
Andrew Harris,
without whose encouragement I never would have come this
far.

Lastly, to my esteemed professors: Steve
Adisasmito-Smith, Chris Henson, Michael Clifton,
Tim Skeen and Samina Najmi,
They taught me the rules, and then told me to break them. I
did.

The Man Who Would Have Been

By
J.J. Mortensen

"It is one thing to write as poet and another to write as a historian: the poet can recount or sing about things not as they were, but as they should have been, and the historian must write about them not as they should have been, but as they were, without adding or subtracting anything from the truth."

— Miguel de Cervantes Saavedra, *Don Quixote*

Prologue

"Truly I was born to be an example of misfortune,
and a target at which the arrows of adversity are aimed."
— Miguel de Cervantes Saavedra, *Don Quixote*

*I check my filthy dashboard clock for the time, then flick
open my heavy gun. 12:47 am. Loaded. Can't remember when. I
probably should have worn a seat-belt on the ride over...oh well.
I take a few dashes of whiskey from my greasy, fingerprint
smeared flask, then tuck it back in my coat's inner-breast pocket.
I cram my snub nose .378 Smith & Wesson revolver in the back of
my belt and slowly finish my cigarette, squinting against the
smoke targeting my eyes as their gaze hovers on the bright light
of the neon sign from across the street shining against the ink
soaked night, disrupting it: El Caballero Muerto. The Dead
Knight. Sounds like a place that's bound to have strong liquor. I
wipe the dripping salt from my forehead with the rough sleeve of
my coat. A lone fly veers through smoke toward my face; I swat it
away and it buzzes off. I roll up the window and shut off the
radio just as Motley Crue's* <u>Wild Side</u> *revs up on my tinny car
audio.*
*   "I hope this doesn't go to shit," I think to myself.
I flick my cigarette into the street; get out of the car, lock it, and
walk across the yellow lines toward the door of the bar.*

Red.

Part I

"And so, to sum it all up, I perceive everything I say as absolutely true, and deficient in nothing whatever, and paint it all in my mind exactly as I want it to be."
— Miguel de Cervantes Saavedra, *Don Quixote*

I

Black.

Bang.

      I started to come to, roused by the sound of a heavy car door slamming just outside of my office on Blackstone, just south of Shaw avenue. I opened my eyes and saw the vast linear desert of my maple desk stretch before me, littered with ruffled papers and notes and ash to the very corners of the earth. After a moment I groaned myself upright in my plush chair and, blinking a few times, I checked the clock on my now visually proportioned desk: 2:18 pm. A bit early in the day for my liking, but not an unreasonable hour for me to do business, so I brushed the bottle of Black Label into my desk drawer, smashed my cigarette in the tray a couple of times, turned off the music I had playing and flipped on my 60 watt overhead office light. As the hollow echo of footsteps approached, nearer the door to my cramped office space, I slapped myself as sober as I could; trying to straighten out my white-ish button up shirt presentably underneath my dark grey cotton overcoat without much luck. It's tough to get slouch wrinkles out just by patting them roughly. I rubbed my hands together in anticipation and surveyed the confined room quickly ensuring it was presentable. Or at least as close as it would come. It was kinda smokey, and the yellowed paint on the walls was cracking like a china vase, which didn't help the subliminal image of a death mask that my office seemed to carry with it. Still, I had worn it proudly since the day I leased it and paid my dues, the day I got my licence; the furniture was nice enough. I heard the staccato tapping of feet on cement crescendo and diminuendo, until silence fell again.

After waiting a stillborn minute, I picked up the remote and turned the stereo back on. Satchmo's rendition of *Summertime* flowed forth. Fuckin' beautiful, I sighed. I became aware of the rotating fan in the back right corner of my office mildly cooling my sticky neck every few seconds and then moving away, grumbling as it looked around the hot room, as though annoyed at having to cool off such a dingy place. I turned it down; listening to the sweet sounds of that horn was more important than staying cool. I pulled the whiskey bottle back out of hiding, threw a few sloshes into my booze hangar, and lit up another stogie, puffing on it like some Wall Street fat cat as the haze invaded the beams of light. I believe that's the politically correct term. I reached around behind my head with my left hand a few times before successfully hitting the switch to the ceiling fixture...and then feeling the deep warmth bathe me, surround me, envelop me...

Red.

I sat in my armchair, dragging on my cigarette, basking in the calm vermillion emanating from the three lamps in my office. One on the desk in front of me, one in the back left corner, and one in the opposite right corner at the front of my office, by the washed out glass front door. I closed my eyes and took a deep breath. I rested my chin on my palm, keeping the lit *cigarillo* near to my mouth for safekeeping.

See, I kept the 60 watt white bulb in the ceiling light to make what few clients ever came around feel more comfortable, like in a shrink's office, but I hated it. I told people the red light was for darkroom development, but I use digital. I'm not an artist. Truth is something about those red light bulbs comforted me, soothed me. I can only say I knew that it was red, but to me...to me red was white. It's the blank slate on which I wrote the story of my life; I would swear it was the color of my dreams if I could remember them. Red is the base palate from which I painted my view of the world over its rigorously black and white dichotomies.

I removed my hand containing the miniature towering inferno from my mouth, and took another long swig from the sacred glass flagon to follow. After my cherished blackout, I wanted to do anything except rest more, but what the hell could I do? Can't run a business if I leave my office; who needed people like me anymore? I'll tell you who: suspicious spouses, protective parents, lawyers, and people trying to find people what don't want to be found. Nosy little weasels.

I inhaled a huge gust from my cigarette, took another fill of drink, and exhaled, watching the smoke swirl around itself, dancing and dissipating; no trace left but an air tinged with decay.

In my line of work, the only people who come for professional advice are people who are about to pay you to tell them what they already think, and definitely don't want to hear. Certainly not from the likes of me. I had never looked into a case of adultery and come back saying, "Well ma'am, your husband has been taking pottery classes to surprise you with a vase for your anniversary", or some crock. It was always me throwing some snapshots of him with another woman down on the desk, a cold "I'm sorry" spewing from my mouth; the passing of the tissues as they blubbered all over my leather chairs (alright, they weren't real leather, but it was nice imitation and I didn't want it wet either), and then the payment in flesh or gold...usually just cash.

The whiskey bottle was still weighing too much for my hand's sake, so I relieved it of a little bit more juice. It soothed my throat with cleansing fire.

If it sounds like I was some kind of callous bastard, let me just say...I didn't enjoy receiving the money any more than I enjoyed the shitty work. I hated my job. I had always imagined that it would be more like in the old noir films, like on television mysteries. Yeah, I foolishly held to the belief that crime, excitement and danger lay in the...honourable... profession of private investigation. I wasn't expecting to be Sherlock Holmes, with my own Moriarty-like arch nemesis to contend with throughout my life. I didn't figure on being so brilliant as to sit behind a chair like Poirot and deduce the manner of the crime without leaving the room. Hell, I would have settled for *Colombo*'s quirky crime solving or even *Police Squad* antics. But instead my life, my career, my dreams became some purgatory in which the promise of excitement lay ever around the corner and stayed there, mocking me.

I took another deep vortex of tobacco in, the menthol blowing winter's wind through my whiskey burnt throat. I blew out gray billows.

I take my job seriously, or as seriously as I can. No coffee breaks, no donuts, just digging and digging, deeper into someone's life until I strike oil. Like a dog after a fuckin' bone. I wanted to solve mysteries, stop criminals. Save people. That, I take seriously. Instead I am stuck doing menial, worthless rat work. I have to. So, over the years I upped my dosage of booze to "forget about it", and I managed to scrape by on the few meagre cases that came hesitantly screeching open my office door, and timidly approaching the desk. I hate them, and I hate the cases.

Honestly, I've been sexually propositioned with more balls than most of these people come with to ask me to do their dirty work for them. Yeah, it's fuckin' dirty work. If you want to find out if your spouse is cheating, call them out on their bullshit to their face; follow them your goddamn self. But listen, before you do that, why don't you go ahead and ask yourself two little questions: If they are cheating, do you want to stay with them? If they're not cheating and you just don't trust them, do you think you should be with them? Someone always ends up a loser in these situations, and if it's some poor guy or gal who doesn't even know that the love of their life pays drunks to follow them around and make sure they're not low-life cheating garbage...I felt worse about doing my job, knowing I hadn't solved anything; all I served to do was exacerbate a problem.

I took a few brisk puffs from the cig. Exhale stage left.

I hated tracking down some poor kid with overbearing parents who they suspect of doing drugs, and finding them smoking pot. I had to report that to their parents as my clients, knowing full well this poor kid had one hell of a day at pre-law school, a night of homework that always gets done lying ahead of 'em, and they're just trying to wind down with some TV and a smoke. Now, on top of all that, having to deal with parents' criticisms and lectures like they're not grown, working towards... fuckin' something.

I sipped from the bottle leisurely. Heavily, but leisurely.

God forbid I got a parent taking up the precious oxygen in my office worried that their kid's drinking around here. I turned into a fuckin' Lewis Black stand-up routine: Drinking? In Fresno?! Yeah! Look it up! Everybody drinks in this godforsaken place! Way too fuckin' much! Don't send your kid to the alcoholic city where dreams go to die. You really need a detective to tell you this shit?! Jesus...

Sometimes I just didn't think people used their fucking heads before coming to me. I liked to be the man you came to when you'd exhausted your resources, not before you'd even run a preliminary internet search. I was supposed to be useful to people with real issues, not some kind of pseudo-legal cop for trivial, first-world problems. Dimwads.

I couldn't believe sometimes that people thought money would just erase any memory of honor. I didn't like being a hound dog for fuckers, sniffing out their kill. The worst of these; I didn't like having to track down exes and other people who've run off within their rights. I always figured they had their reasons, and whether or not their reasons were good enough to the client, or good enough to me, I figure they were sufficient to the runner to make them act upon it (which is more than I can say for a lot of people in this country. I mean you have the freedom, but you just sit in your shitty little situation till you die? What the fuck for?). But, sometimes money is tight, and I had to take a case on, whether I liked it or not. Go ahead, call me a hypocrite. Who isn't?

A loose fly flitted about the window, flying in and out of the wrought iron bars as though it were attempting to complete an obstacle course. Heh heh. It was driving like me: drunk. It flew around the door and windows, seeing the illusory exit as well as its felled comrades on the sill below it, but not sure how to proceed. It started loitering around the dartboard I keep in the front of the office. I picked up a red dart from my desk, and threw.

Bang.

I missed the fly. 13 points. Which is good, cause I was tired of patching over the drywall from all the times I had thrown a dart too early, too sober, or too drunk. Which was generally too often. Ah, who am I kidding, I never fixed anything around the office, it was falling apart. I had no idea how many code violations there were but no one ever came by to ask, and despite always wanting to have been a craftsman, I just never found the time for it.

Countless times I had tracked some poor woman down for her ex, wondering later whether or not I had fucked up; wondering if his innocent worry for her well being, and his pathetic hope to work it out was all an act. Maybe he was conning me, and he was really here to hurt her. I mean, my job was done when it's done. I can't go after my clients or targets after the job is done; it's unprofessional. But in the back of my mind, I had always hoped that I never led some poor soul back to torment, or to death. Love is a curious thing. I've seen people kill themselves, kill others, sometimes even kill the one they love just to hold onto them forever like some sick, Browningesque, poetic twist. It makes people commit to someone for a lifetime; it makes people lie to each other. Love is red. Red is the heat fucking madness in the brain.

I finished my smoke, reached around for the pack on the desk without opening my eyes, threw a few cigarettes on the desk and lit up another one. I tossed the carton back down on the sticky paper landing pad.

The fly kept the motor turning. I opened my eyes, and shot.

Bang.

Double 10. Still the enemy eludes me, shuffling about elsewhere, hidden but heard.

I never took on a case if I thought the client wasn't being straight with me about something, but I couldn't always be sure. Had a few times I ran into a client where I'm looking into the target. Generally when the two paths crossed like that, not only did I not believe in coincidence, I didn't believe in their bullshit anymore and I demanded answers. First politely, then decreasingly so. Hey, if they fired me they still had a bill to settle, and if they pressed charges, I had a friend in the department. My only friend, actually.

I took another few sips from the slowly warming whiskey, then took a few drags on the cig. I turned off the lights, leaned back in my chair and closed my eyes, and listened intently to the sweet fanfares of the trumpet ebbing into my auditory. I breathed in the nicotine fog as acutely as I could.

Black.

Bang.

Somewhere a door shut.

"Mr. Morris?"

The voice rang through in the smoky darkness. Was that me? Was I Morris? Or was I calling him? It didn't sound like one of the voices I was used to hearing. I didn't open my eyes for an elongated moment. I strained against my mind, as if psychically, to glean my surroundings...a bar? My office? Motel? What the hell time was it? Was I wearing clothes?

"Detective Jon Morris?", the woman repeated a little louder.

I took a chance, and opened my eyes, rubbing at the gum in the corners. She was standing there, just inside the doorway to my office. Her silhouette was outlined by the dirty yellow glow of the streetlamps out on the sidewalk outside, which cast a glow around her body like Our Lady of Guadalupe. Holy, lovely. Pure.

My ipod had run through my collection of Pops' greatest hits, and he had swung back around to *When You're Smilin'*. The upbeat swing of the tempo helped get my mind moving as I drew this woman in with my eyes. I couldn't believe it. Was it her? A part of me knew that it couldn't be and yet, for a moment, my mind let my heart convince my eyes that she was standing there again, just like she once had. My eyes began to adjust to the lighting, and I realized I had better adjust myself as well, or else lose a client. Never a good thing.

I scootched my ass back into my chair, bounced in it a bit, getting myself settled and throwing the dead filter between my fingers on the stained carpet beneath my desk. I drank in this strange woman. Her silken looking top was cherry red; I saw it first as my eyes adjusted. I could see that she was wearing tight, tastefully ripped boot-cut jeans. I could see the shape of her cream carved legs. She looked about 5 foot 1; a nice height, and a figure to match. Her body arched at just the right moments for the eye to slice along her edges. Her hips swung hypnotically, yet unconsciously, from side to side as she made her way over to stand just barely before my desk, still lingering in the middle of the room. I leaned upward, taking her in better, and dragged my hand across my chin.

One shoulder strap over her right shoulder led down and across to where shirt met shirt, over her curving breasts, slithering under her left arm. I got a whiff of jasmine. I thought she might have been a hooker, I get them sometimes when business on the strip is slow, various complaints: robbed by a john, tired of their pimp and looking for a case to take to the cops behind his back, just trying to get some other whore that fought her for a corner nabbed. I never took those, either because I didn't care or I knew the money was always crap. I wasn't sure whether to tell this dame to stay or go, if that was the case.

I flipped on the red, and then the dull white overhead. It was then that I saw her eyes. I started openly. No, not her eyes; her eyes were hazel, it was the flecks within. Absinthe, with as much expression, sorrow, and something illuminating them from within. Something about them spoke to me, softened me. "Yes?" I said, hoarsely, standing to greet her properly (and confining the whiskey to its drawer again). "I'm Private Detective Jon Morris ma'am. Uh, I apologize. I dozed off for a while and thought I, uh, might have been dreaming." I chuckled and smiled at her gently, motioning for her to sit down in the chair across from mine. I checked the desk clock: 6:24 pm. I was wearing clothes. Excellent. "What can I do for you miss...?".

"Anna Llorena," she replied. She sat down. Her voice was smooth, timid. She had a gorgeous Spanish accent, by which I mean the language, not the country. Not too strong, but just enough to roll my r's around a bit. I just couldn't tell where she was from exactly. She struggled in the right hand chair across from the vodka filled glass on my desk. Looks like water, so I figured no one will get suspicious immediately. "Miss Llorena." I echoed. "That's a beautiful name." "Please, call me Anna", she said, quietly. She continued squiggling, and brushed her mahogany colored hair away from her mocha face with her fingers, making furtive eye contact with me as she shifted uncomfortably in her chair. She was nervous about coming to me, understandably. Most people are.

"Alright Anna, what seems to be the trouble?"

"I...I want to hire you to find my brother." She quivered softly.

"Well, Miss Llorena..." I boasted.

"Anna." Almost a gust of wind in my ears.

I reiterated hesitantly, speaking her name aloud. "Anna, do you mind if I smoke?" I asked her permission, not wanting to make her any more uncomfortable. I picked up a single off the desk, and grabbed my lighter from my pocket.

"It's your office." she droned, almost expressionlessly.

"Well, thank you, miss, but that wasn't the question at hand." I gave her a wry smile from the left corner of my mouth.

She smiled gently back, looking at me, letting me look into her eyes again. Her voice came to life again, like notes of an overture after a long rest; alto-soprano:

"No, Mr. Morris, I do not mind if you smoke. See, the trouble is..."

I interrupted, cigarette hanging out of my mouth as I lit it.

"Would you care for one?", as I inhaled breathlessly. I picked another single up and held it out to her.

"No, thank you Mr. Morris. Please, I need you to find..."

"Jon." I put the cigarette down.

"What?" she looked confused.

"You can call me Jon." I smoked intently.

"Very well, Jon I am desper..."

"Anna," I interrupted again, "I understand you are upset and you want a solution to your troubles. However, I am going to need more than just your last name and a sex to find your brother; I need to know, from you, calmly, exactly what happened that caused you to seek out professional help looking for your brother and why it is the police haven't been able to help you". I took a drink from the glass in front of me and shifted my weight, worried that this case might be shit. I assuaged my fears with another take of smoke.

"I'm sorry." She said, quietly. "I'm not sure of anything, I just know that my brother and I talk every day, and he hasn't responded to any of my texts or picked up my calls for two days and yesterday I went around to his place and he was go-o-o-ne!", she spit out with all of her breath, like a deflating air mattress. She started to weep, and I could see the fear. Fear of what I wasn't sure. Maybe she wasn't either.

"No, please, Anna, no reason to be sorry," I said, uncharacteristically putting out my cigarette, getting up and moving around my desk to give her a tissue and comfort her. "You need help; you're concerned. I understand." I put my arm around her, and squeezed her gently, in a manner which I thought comforting. "But, I wouldn't be doing my job if I jumped up and started poking around all of fuckin' Fresno without getting more information first, making sure that I can even help you with the problem." I chuckled falsely, hoping to lighten her up as well.

She nodded, and wiped her eyes. I handed her another tissue; she was sniffling.

"Thank you Detective". She spoke weakly.

"Jon." I reminded her.

"Jon", she whispered.

I walked back around and took my notebook out of the drawer from beside the bottle of rum, and grabbed one of a few blue pens lying around at the bottom. I picked up another cigarette and fired it up.

"Could I have a glass of water?" she dabbed about her lips with her small tongue, wiping her eyes with her silky arms.

I put my notebook and pen down and popped the cig between my teeth. I walked over to the bookshelf where I kept a few glass bottles and tumblers next to the CD's, you know, class the place up a bit? I grabbed one of the chiselled glass tumblers, and poured her a glass of water, breathing through the cigarette, exhaling from the other side of my mouth.
"I'm sorry, it's room temp, would you like some ice?" I opened the mini-fridge and grabbed the tray, brushing off a few loose crystals onto the rug.
"Please." She looked quite unnerved.
I dropped a few cubes and walked to her, and handed her the glass, slowly perspiring in our hands as I made the pass. She took it, and sipped gently, but thirstily. I walked back around and thrust myself into my chair, picking up my notebook and pen in one deft, drunken motion.

"Why don't you begin by telling me why you think your brother is missing?".

Red.

I felt the tips of my fingers getting warmer. I opened my eyes, and extinguished the culprit in the apocalyptic looking ashtray. The ceiling light was dark. She was gone. I don't know what happened to the fly, maybe he left with her. I didn't hear it anymore, so I assumed I would have peace of mind now. I picked up the last dart and chucked it half-heartedly.

Bang.

17.

I needed another drink, so I grabbed my tumbler on the desk, still half full. *Cabaret* was playing on the stereo now, and Louis Armstrong was speaking to me, telling me of the sweet chaos of the world. I drank to that. Well, I drank for a lot of fucking reasons, but that one suited me well enough in the moment. I took out my canister, grinder and papers, and rolled myself a couple of joints. I didn't chain smoke them like some teenage stoner, I just smoked a couple joints over the day; kept my nerves calm. It wasn't a medical reason *per se*, but I didn't do well when I got riled up and the smoking helped. Told the "doctor" I had back pain from sleeping in my office chair. Truth is it was migraines from having to drink myself to sleep, but it usually was in the chair, or the tub. Occasionally the floor. At least I thought the migraines were from daily alcohol poisoning. I spent money on a nice plush red armchair after the 5th time I passed out in my office.

The weed counteracted the negative effects of the booze. It made me eat, kept my temper under control, and added to the positive effects, namely: keep on forgetting. I lit up one of the more poorly rolled ones, and inhaled sharply, then slowly. I held it, as though maybe if I kept it in, maybe it would stay, maybe I would stop breathing altogether, and just fade off into...I coughed, gave a few, then inhaled. Nice, smooth.

Mack the Knife came on, and I snapped my fingers to the rhythm with my left hand, right still feeding me smoke. After a few puffs, I sat back in my seat, closed my eyes. I reached around the wheels of my chair for the whiskey bottle, and grabbed the rum instead. That worked fine by me, as long as I stick with dark for the night. The liquor, I mean. I took a drink, and my sea legs took me over to the stereo. It took a minute to focus my sight, and I scrolled through the jazz selections. Wynton Marsalis, ladies and gentlemen, *Sleepytime Down*

South. I walked back to my desk and set myself down behind it, drinking most of the way. I set the bottle down on the desk next to a few ciggies and the black darts. I grabbed one. I looked up, across the room. I saw red. I saw a circle. I saw a red circle.

Bang.

The circle was vanquished. I sat, victorious in my throne, champion of the rings, conqueror of the evil eye and scourge of poorly structured bar walls on occasion. I pulled on my j, blackening my lungs with a sweet high. I chugged down whiskey for a few seconds, then fell back into the waiting arms of my love, my chair.

Black.

"Nngggphhhhuuuuu…" I continued with a few harsh coughs. Red warmed me as I came back from the abyss, wrapping me in a mantle of light. I opened my eyes. I closed them again as sweat stung them, and blinked them clear. I was burning in hell. It was so hot, so empty…just light and dark and me. I think three's a crowd, and light and dark have known each other longer…I should just go…the light through the grimy cage on my windows held me there, making me watch. I don't want to see, I want the light to go, so I can be alone. Alone in the dark, alone in my thoughts… myself. My thoughts have always been the only company I need. They've never confused me, or lied to me, or deceived me. All my thoughts do is ground and center me, give me focus, give me purpose.

Red.

Shit...the client. I have a case. I have a bloody case, it's...who...her...missing....Shit! I needed to recover, so I plucked the bottle of rum from my lap and took a few deep breaths from it. Ah. I remembered then, just barely...fuzzily. Her brother...Rick? I turned quickly and whacked the lanky rotating fan on to its highest setting, feeling the relief as it slowly drowned out the dry Fresno heat.

I didn't know him, or her, or anyone she had mentioned, and I didn't want to. I didn't need to. This case was not interesting, it was even premature; he hadn't even actually been missing for a day. There must have been something, something other than those emerald shards glowing like phosphorus in her eyes which made me say yes to this. Those soulful eyes...they pleaded with me to help, but didn't beg. She didn't need me because she couldn't do this herself, she needed me because she wouldn't bring herself to. Something about the nature of her worry, and her need to keep distant stirred me; I related to that. I worried about people. Not specific people, not people I knew or thought I'd seen, but people I knew existed, somewhere out there...abstracts.

I brought the bottle to my lips again. One small splash. Damn. I arched my back in my seat and grabbed a loose cigarette off of the edge of my desk. I tried to light it; had to turn away from the uppity fan and cover the flame. I started smoking it, and picked up another black dart. The clock on my desk read 7:39 pm.

Bang.

I stood up and stretched, and checked my coat and then pants pockets for cash. Upon finding some, I trudged across the carpet and grabbed my pre-tied necktie off of the erect red dart sticking awkwardly out of the board and threw it over my greased back hair hanging slovenly around my ears. I walked out my office door and headed left into the hot, muggy night air that engulfed me.

I worried about kids, especially the ones who live in shit neighbourhoods. Punks these days were as desperate as they were stupid, which always made for a violent combination. Parents didn't know how to raise their kids in today's world. I worried about the people who were losing their jobs and didn't even have an office chair to pass out in. I worried about people getting harassed, or persecuted for handicap or sex or race or some such stupid, ignorant, bigoted shit. With all the people to hate in the world, all the people who give plenty of reason to hate them, it just seemed pointless to be prejudiced, to be so...judgemental. Judge worth, and nothing else; base it on merit, intelligence, class and deed. But not in this world. Ha. Never here. Here, I guess these townies had nothing better to occupy their time than drinking, drugs and hate. Here, that was all there was, for them...for me.

I arrived at the liquor store there, just a few doors down from my office. The window was littered with luminous ads, cheap liquor, energy drinks, low grade tobacco, snuff...for a minute I thought I caught myself looking at myself in the window, but then it was gone.

The people browsing were nothing much to admire. It looked to me like they didn't even know how to dress themselves. ROSS has dress shirts and slacks, ya know; it's not hard to look human. I worried about all these fucktards who are getting too stupid for their own good, for any of our good. People around here are almost too stupid to forgive. I may have hated them for their seemingly intentional unawareness, but it was hard to blame them when I pitied them so much, wandering about like zombies. I don't know if it was parents, the horrible schools, or just their own base nature that put them here. I may not have made what I had dreamed out of my life, but at least I chased that small dream, vigorously. Unlike so many in this world who simply settled into their sad realities, never fighting, never trying...never evolving...

The alcohol selections there in the store were good; I went with Jameson, Kraken, and Skyy. Bottles, all except for the Kraken. I always got a handle of that shit. I'm a whiskey man, but that shit is great. I paid in cash at the counter, and asked for a pack of menthol 100's as well. The cashier gave them to me, and gave me a look I didn't think I liked, but they were always nice to my face, so I let it go. I paid in cash and dropped the change in the take-a-penny tray. I always did, regardless of the amount. Hate loose change jingling. The place ding-donged at me as I left. I hate that noise too.

Now, I was worried about Anna too. And she was worried about this brother of hers. Why? I had no idea...still. What had he gotten into? Did she know, and just wasn't telling me? Maybe she honestly wanted me to find out what happened to him, but I can't think why she would...think something is out of place, and not... share it with me.

I walked back to my office, set the bag of goodies on the floor next to my desk, and stripped the bag downward. I shuffled clumsily around my desk for any notes I might have taken. I always take meticulous notes if I can just remember what I wrote them on. Nothing useful on the yellow notepad. The sketch pad had a mediocre drawing of a tree with a noose, but nothing sparked me from that; I was probably trying to draw while watching a Clint Eastwood film. Ah...my leather bound notebook. It had been a gift from...someone...someone I had once cared about. I flipped through the pages, the dog ears, the sticky notes...Ricardo Llorena, Rick. Ricky. 28 years old, five foot seven, dark hair, brown eyes. Tanned, light facial hair. Ah, a picture, good. Damn, I had just used post-its to keep it in place on the page. Oh well, it seemed to be staying.

I opened the bottle of whiskey. The vodka would end up in the freezer, I rarely drank it, but now and then I needed to drink something other than whiskey and rum, and no cheap brandy was gonna fuckin' cut it.

Rick had a record, but not for anything someone would end up missing over. Just some drunk and disorderlies, assault, but no weapons charges. If he had done any time she hadn't told me, but I would check it out just the same. In any event Ricky was small time, he probably just owed some people money; had to work it off by having to run jobs for them till he paid up. Nothing too serious, debt. Even with the drugs and weapons trade, there's less violence than the media likes to make out. Everyone falls short now and then, but you only waste rats and loose cannons, otherwise it's a beating for a warning. But from what I could make out from my notes, he wasn't either. Good kid, good brother, took care of his sister, hangs out with a diverse crowd, and recently spent more time out of the house. It makes sense with Anna being more independent and going to school for pre-med and all.

But then why did I take the case? I think I took it because people only worry when they are afraid, and people are only afraid when they are in danger, or at least they think they are. I had been dying for danger. This case didn't scream it, but it whispered it to me, softly, while a voice in my head told me that this case would be just as humdrum as them all, that I would never find the case I was waiting for. But still, that sweet seduction seeped into my head, and I bought it. I knew, this case... it was gonna be the one.

I took off towards the address Anna had given me for her brother.

Black

Red.

It sees me. From across the room
it watches me, telling me everything is
fine, lying to me
sweetly,
sickly.
I think it knows I know.
I think it knows I don't trust it.
It's crazy, some malfunctioning machine. It glows, even in the
dark, I see it.
I would call it a sociopath, but...it isn't human.
Hal. Come to kill me, come from the past, and the future, and
even sprung from the confines of fiction to torment me.
Then he is silent.

Then I am alone.

Still the eye watches, but says nothing. The emptiness of space.
Dave?
Dave?
I call out.
Dave's not here, man...

Hello? The eye, I have to hit the eye.

Bang.

20, in the 3 ring: 60.

Ring.
Ring.
Ring.
Is someone gonna FUCKING GET THAT!?

Hello?

The voice is gone, the voice is gone, gone gone gone...

*I am alone. I am alone with my red and my drink and my dark
and I have a case.*
Anna.
*FUCK! The ringing in my fucking ears!!! Something she had said,
must have set something off in my mind, through the tunnels, as
my thoughts scurry like rats, never coming to me fast enough,
never quite sure if they're heading in the right direction.*
Here's the cheese.

*Here it is, come to me, bring me the piece I'm missing LET ME
SEE WHAT I NEED TO FUCKING SEE!*

*Why can't I see it, why can't I have it, why can't I figure it all
out!?!*

Black.

II

Black.

I opened my eyes. My notebook was in my left hand lying draped on top of the rough, green shag carpet, along with my small flashlight. My revolver was in the other, clutched against my chest. The foreign tattered couch beneath me smelled vaguely of piss and vomit. About those general pastel colors too. I checked, and it wasn't my doing. Good. I struggled to sit up, and pocketed my gun in my coat pocket. I looked around the room. Lights of cars passing on the street shined through the blinds like an old moving picture, flashing strobing lights around the vicinity. I hadn't been in this house before, so I assumed it was Ricky's. Or...well, hoped. I looked around, and it seemed to match what I had expected. It was little nicer, actually. I couldn't remember anything about getting here, so I looked at my notebook. Open. Blank. Shit. How the fuck did I get this address? She gave it to me...I flipped back to my last notes. Nothing added. I checked my phone: 8:07 pm. I figured I must not have searched the place yet, so I moved to get to work snooping around, judging the family pictures on the wall, the decor, looking in his underwear drawer and medicine cabinet. As I stood up, a small yellow note fluttered to the crusty stained carpet like the last leaf that falls before the winter kill. It read:

Slick's.
10 pm Friday.

Hm. Great. A bar, a time. Not too helpful of a clue. I tucked the flashlight in the crook of my arm and whipped out my cigarettes and lighter. The end ignited, and I smoked according to standard procedure: Long drawn gasps of smoke until I'm quite certain I've had enough, then leisurely absorb the smoke from the corner of my mouth until it's dead.

I started meandering about the place again, trying another go at finding something useful. I shined my light around the room in my left hand, smoking with my right. Pictures of family and a couple friends. Blankets on a chair in the corner. A decent television set and stereo sitting on a pretty nice entertainment center. It was the classiest piece of furnishing in the room, but hardwood shit is expensive. Canvassing the floor was an oriental looking area rug, some ash, a few bits of popcorn, and a piece of red lint beneath the dark coffee table which sat on it. Nothing but trash on the table, maybe an old magazine here and there.

The smoke became a little thick on my tongue, so I removed the cig momentarily, breathed in dirty Fresno air, then stuck my piece right back where it belonged.

I moved through the door on the right side of the room by the front door into the cramped kitchen. It wasn't clean, but there weren't any bugs scurrying about. Noticeably, at least. The sink was full of dirty dishes on one side, but not in such a way that cried for help. I ashed my cigarette in it. To the right, the fridge had sticky notes, postcards held with magnets, and some odd assortments of illegible scraps of paper. I noticed a conspicuous square of clean white. I must have grabbed the note from there and immediately hit the couch. I looked for a work schedule, but didn't find one. Must have regular work. Or maybe work he didn't want a public record of it. Or maybe...I'm just suspicious. I opened the fridge and a wave of cool and stink exhumed itself; cheese, milk, catsup, mustard, leftover Denny's container and a 6 pack with 4 beers left. Freezer had some vegetables. Ice cream. Bread in the cupboard. Ramen. Soy sauce and a few cans of chili (con carne). The drawers were fairly empty. Just some cheap silverware; leftover sauce packets from fast food places. In the corner across from the outdated stove was a sturdy looking card table with a few dirty dishes and a bunch of envelopes. A small plastic chair stood by, its mate in the far corner. I shuffled the mail around on the table, looking for the best piece. No postcards, no letters, no paychecks, just bills for insurance and utilities. His insurance plan was not comprehensive.

I tripped my way over some dirty towels lying on the floor into the bedroom, and dropped my cigarette on the rug.

Fuck it; I stomped around, made sure it was out. I left the butt. The place smelled dank. The orange sheets on his twin bed were crumpled about, as though he had been tossing and turning in his sleep just before I arrived. I shined my light around. Posters. Lil' Wayne, Chingon, Ill Niño, AC/DC, Metallica, Five finger Death Punch, Scarface, and a few Playboy spreads lined the upper walls. Lower he had a few photos of him with family. He was younger in the pictures, but one with his sister and a middle aged woman (I assumed to be their mother) looked recent, judging from Anna's appearance. I scratched at an itch on my ear, just where the lobe met my ill-cropped sideburns. His desk was littered with chip bags, fast food wrappers of a varied assortment, and what appeared to be an 8th. or thereabouts. His bong was sitting right there on the desk. Ah, what the hell, it looked like good shit. I opened the plastic satchel, and was hit with a wave of evergreen. I tore some of the frosty, gummy leaves from their stems and packed them in the bowl. He had a lighter sitting just under a burger wrapping, so it saved me the time of searching for mine. I lit up. Nice...

As I felt myself become lifted, I started to think...this guy didn't have expensive shit or hard drugs. I puffed again, and put the bong down. I paced the room, looking about, hoping to get to know Ricky without ever having to meet him. I tossed his closet. Only things I found there were a bunch of sneakers, gym shorts, t-shirts, jeans. Nothing too expensive, but he dressed well to fit his lifestyle. I shined my light in the bathroom, and stepped in, half opening drawers and checking the cabinets. Toothbrush, paste, comb, mouthwash, Old Spice deodorant, some kind of designer aftershave, I didn't stop to read it. Nothing odd. No drugs. Now that's odd. Everybody's got aspirin or Tylenol or something they never threw out from ages before. But there was nothing here.

I went back to the desk, packed and took another hit from the bong. Underneath the mat he used for marijuana was a book. It looked like a yearbook. I gently slid the mat to the opposite corner of the desk, and looked. It was an old green banker's ledger. I opened it. His handwriting was almost as bad as mine, but I made out what I could.

Walmart, at the beginning of the month.
Red Wave.
Rent.
Ghaeleb's.
Insurance.
What I assume are Camels from CVS, judging by the price.
Jimbo's.
Power.
Ate out a few times.
Music or movies from Rasputin.

Across from each scratched in location, there was a figure, presumably expenses. On each of the lines across from the name of a bar was a number. An obscenely high number. $475 at the El Caballero Muerto. Unbelievable. $150. Red Wave. $250 at Jimbo's. $525 at El Caballero Muerto. $350 El Caballero Muerto. $75, Red Wave. $500, El Caballero Muerto.

The book read much the same up 'til the last page the author had written in. I flipped back to previous months, and his lifestyle seemed consistent. Looks like my mark was a bit of a barfly. Or maybe a bar runner. Launder money through a bar, hardly ever gets caught by the IRS. And cops in this city are as attentive as the mothers, the DEA about as effective. Where to start? El Caballero Muerto? No, if he was putting that much money into that place, maybe his disappearance was about where he got it from, not where he took it. I copied down a few of the bar names and figures into my notebook. I walked back into the living room, and took a last look around. Nothing to tell me where he was, where he might be, where the hell he would have taken off to without alerting his sister. Nothing...

Black.

I became lucid about halfway to this bar I was heading to. Or maybe it was a club. Shit. The lights hurt my eyes as I started trying to regain my bearings. Leaves crunched under my feet softly, every now and then. They fluttered around my feet and legs in the warm gusts of wind which haunted the valley. I was walking down Blackstone, not far from my office. Ok...just past Herndon...the place should be somewhere around here on the left side of the street...I think...? The cars drove past loudly. The incessant rumbling hurt my head, each whiz a missed note, the occasional horn honking an abrasion to the melody.

Ahead of me a strange slender figure stretched out, following me, mimicking my every move and then jumping about cartoonishly as the illumination from the street lamps caught me from different angles. I thought of that imp, Peter Pan. That mischievous fucking shadow. I laughed out loud to myself, and my shadow danced as I did, as if sensing my humor and expounding it, stretching it to delight. The notes of my laughter were drowned out by the bass of passing traffic. The pockmarked cement beneath my feet which banged with every step, that concrete wasteland which stretched forth until my feet forgot the earth, lived solely on sediment rock forged by man.

Cities were built to roar with enough noise and people to distract you from how overwhelming it is, not just cram all the traffic and shops onto three major fucking streets to give me a headache. Whatever. At least here people understood that honking is a useless attack on the rest of their slow-witted, fast driving brethren.

I pulled out my cigs from my pocket, and flicked my lighter at it a few times. I got it, and pocketed the lighter again. A man who appeared to be homeless approached me. He was wearing a dirty black-ish hoodie with a red flannel coat over it, or maybe it was a combo jacket. His brown beard looked like it hadn't been cut in weeks.

"Hey man, you got another?" Smelled like booze and piss. I could relate.

"Yeah." I got two out for him, and flicked my lighter again.

"Thanks." He stood there, leaning toward my light to smoke one, and placed the other on the oily shelf of matted hair behind his right ear.

"No problem." I pocketed my lighter. As I did so, I felt bullets. I stopped, felt around for a minute. Nothing. I shook my right leg. Ah, there we are; that familiar weight. Ankle's easier to reach when sitting on a chair. Barstool...not so much. But since most people don't like to chat about their shady business exchanges surrounded by loudmouth drunks, I figured a booth would be preferable. Who the fuck was this guy I was going to see again?

The homeless guy had been watching my little jig with a curious expression, as I had explained none of this to him. He was too polite to say anything but, "Yeah...thanks for the nicotine man..." and took off at a fair gallop.

Eh, fuck it. I fumbled around at my pockets. My notes just had some bar name that was middle Eastern, I don't know how to pronounce it. Started with a "G". I didn't know why I was armed, I just kept getting this bad feeling about this case, like it was so small, it had to be something. I guess even in my other states, I manage to look after myself alright.

I passed by a stretch of restaurants. Through the windows littered with flashing signs and meal posters, I could see through to a time past. Families having dinner together, friends laughing and enjoying each other's company and conversation in person, young couples on dates gazing across the table at each other, old couples who barely look at each other but when the meal ends, he pulls out her chair and helps her up silently, and holds her hand as they leave, smiling mutedly, as though they share more secrets than I could ever even learn in a lifetime. I saw people...for a moment I caught a glimpse of my warped reflection in the shine of the windows. Then it was gone. Back to the concrete, the metal, the false bravado of the distant businesses followed by like minded sheep...people, they liked to be considered in this part of the world.

Red.

I came to a crossing and the light was red. I didn't mind waiting, I never do. A few minutes to enjoy the stillness before going back to running around like heart surgeons, and people complain about the pause. If anything in your life is hinging on 5 fucking minutes, it has to be very good, or really terrible, and somehow I doubt everyone's got that much going on at all times. I lit up a smoke and looked at the telephone pole to my right. A few unknown bands coming to a local venue that has the room to book an ensemble in front of an audience of more than a dozen. Lost dog. Lost dog. Lost cat. Tutor for math and science ($8 an hour; ridiculous). EDM event. Study abroad in Spain. Underground hip-hop show. Surrounding were a plethora of ink, staples, and tattered edges of papers long torn, burnt or washed away. I wondered if they were torn down because they moved on to bigger and better, or because they fell flat.

A man came, and stood adjacent to me. He was dressed in a brown suit, nicely tailored. His face was a dark black, and his smile was slight, and friendly. He didn't speak to me for a moment, then he cleared his throat even as he began speaking. "You know these things'll kill ya." His voice was smooth, with a touch of gravel and a moderately heavy South African accent. Deep.

I moved my cigarette away from him. "Oh, I'm sorry sir."

"No, it's alright son, I smoke myself. It's just I lost my wife to them, that's all. I figure if it ain't killed me yet, then the good Lord ain't ready for me... yet." He chuckled, then coughed a little. His eyes lit up when he talked about his wife. "You are married?"

"No, sir. I almost was...once."

"Mmm. Sometimes, it's better to almost, and to let it go there. There are some doors you can't ever turn back from." He coughed.

"And there are the doors you stand in front of in your dreams, and wonder what would have happened if you had walked through it, knowing you never can." I puffed harder on my cigarette, still blowing the smoke away from him.

"Sometimes, there's a bigger door than the one you're in front of. But sometimes you can't see it there, 'cause you've got your nose pressed against the door you want so badly, all the ones around you seem out of sight."

"Sometimes." I flicked away my cigarette.

"You seem down, son. Life has got you down?"

"Life...Yes sir, that does seem to be the trouble."

"Have you heard the good news?"

The light changed to green, the brite-lite white man started a-walking, and I started down my same path; the man, waiting for his turn.

"Yeah." I shouted back. "We're all gonna die someday."

"Hallelujah!" he shouted, "and we will be with the good Lord in Heaven!"

I waved, looking back slightly and nodding.

Heaven. Good. Lord. I wish I understood those concepts. I admired this man's faith, even in the face of loss. He had something to cling to, something to hold on to. His door gave him peace. Mine: restlessness.

I always try to be respectful to my elders. I mean obviously not everyone older deserves the respect. But until they give you a fucking reason, you fucking remember that they've done something you haven't. Survived. Oh sure, my generation had done a decade. Ok two. Hit three and it was easy street. Some of these old folks remembered the first depression, the recession came and they laughed while we all shit our pants wondering how we'd do it. But these old fucks did it. They lived to 60, 70...100 some. And here I am damn near dead every night; can't even survive the day. Cause this isn't. Surviving, I mean. Old people smile. Old people feel. Old people are still people, still alive. To them, living in a haze of dementia or alzheimer's is even still living, reminiscent and revealing of their true experience. My haze is of my own doing, my own quiet suicide. Every day, to kill the man I was, so that I can never become him. I can never be broken.

Black.

I was sitting in a booth in the bar. Well, it was sort of a hookah lounge/dance club, more like. The lighting was dim, but colourful. Mirrors lined the walls, refracting and reflecting the beams of green, blue and red around the place, shining in every dark corner. In front of me was a Jack and Coke, an empty shot glass and an empty Guinness bottle. I don't know what I waved at him to get in, but I guess the bouncer was second guessing the decision, cause he was eyeing me like he wanted to take me home, and I was assuming he didn't. I knew I was fucked up, but I had a job to do. I jumped upright and leaned back against the blue vinyl seat, breathing in deeply. "Just keep it together man."

I found my phone in my jacket: 8:51 pm. I put it back and took out my leather bound notebook and put it on the cheap laminated plasterboard table, and looked for my last notes. Here we go...Alright, Ricky had been spending a lot of money here, and I wanted to find out if he was paying someone off, distributing drug profits, or maybe there was some sort of prostitution ring that was run through bars. I didn't see any conspicuous whores. The place had a few fake plants by booths and in corners, which the lights on the ceiling shone through. The air in here smelled fresh, a false freshness though; too filtered and synthetic. Still, it cooled me off. The breeze was contaminated with tropical smoke and mint.

This town was never gonna pull itself up; no amount of Philharmonic concerts and art galleries downtown, or all the pretentious wine bars in the Tower District could undo the weight that held this place in an intellectual and moral sub-terrain. The great pretenders, these cowardly barbarians, always feigning what they perceived as class and progress which the rest of the world just saw as some strange caricature of humanity. Never thinking that no one's ever heard of this town, no one's ever gonna hear of them, either. They are content to be nothing and live as nobody for the rest of their days, anywhere on the face of this planet, so pathetically desperate to live any way they can that they barely live at all. Pick a side, cowards.

The bartender was this big, Persian looking fucker, possibly Armenian, sporting a short sleeve Hawaiian shirt and moustache to match. He was about 6 foot 2, looked like a working man. Not heavy, per se, but built. He was chatting with one of the guys sitting at the bar; seemed to have a friendly demeanour about him. I relocated and sat down at the opposite end of the bar. He walked my way, past a plethora of varied bottles, filled to different levels, still chatting with the patron down the bar.

"How's it going?" He said with a slight accent. His demeanor was business, but not unfriendly toward me.

"Alright, and you?"

"Not too bad, what can I get for you now my friend? The same?" he said hoarsely, smiling.

"Mid-shelf whiskey shot and a Jack and Coke, my good man."

"Pepsi alright for you?" He looked at me.

"Yeah that's fine."

"Back in a minute" He headed off to the bottles and hoses just down the way and mixed up my drink; came back over.

Bang.

"I'll be right back with your shot sir."

"Thanks."

I sat, looking around. Place was pretty lively, lots of people dancing, smoking, the music was good. I don't go in for club and techno and dance and all that fucking computer music, but still...it had melody. The lights on the ceiling shone down on people faces as though in a sci-fi film, illuminating cheekbones from one angle and dark eyes from another. Perhaps the appeal lay in not being able to see others, but to have a shifting lens through which to view them, never seeing them as they truly are. The smoke only added to the effect of their deformed selves on display.

Bang.

"Here you are."

"Thanks." I put a $10 down on the bar. "Hey?"

"Yes?" He didn't look up from the register.

"I was wondering if you could help me out, I'm trying to find someone who hangs out here, but I don't see him here tonight." He pushed over my change.

"We get a lot of people man, I don't really know most of them by face; we only have a few regulars who come in daily."

"Well this guy came in weekly or so, I just figure maybe you might know who he hangs with or what he does." I pushed the change back toward him.

I took out the picture Anna had given me and laid it down on the bar.

Without looking, "I don't think I know him man, he may have been in here a few times."

"You sure?" I looked him in the eye.

"Yes sir." He looked away, began cleaning glasses or some such unnecessary task.

"Cause he spends a few hundred a week here." I urged.

"Yes, sir, he comes in now and then and buys lots of drinks for all the pretty girls and for his friends." He wiped down the bar, vigorously.

"Oh, so you do know him?" I intoned, implying deceit on his part.

"No, he comes in, I see him, he orders drinks, I serve the drinks, he pays, he leaves. I do not know him." The bartender was becoming exasperated with my questions, so I thought I would take a different approach.

"I just want to know if you've seen him recently is all. He's not in trouble, I'm a detective; his family's worried, they haven't heard from him in a bit, I know he hangs out here, I just want to know if you know where I can find him? Is he mixed up in something shady?"

The bartender just shook his head. I didn't know if he was answering no, or just still refusing to give me anything.

"Can I see some I.D.?" He said, looking at me sideways.

"Of course." I took out my wallet and flipped it open.

"That's not a badge". He said, becoming more wary of me.

"No, it's a licence."

"Where's your badge?" He started tensing up.

"I'm not a cop."

"You said you were a detective. I can't just blab customers' shit all over for nothing man, I'll lose business." He started backing away from me, so as to let people see he wasn't getting too chummy.

"I'm a private investigator." I took one of my business cards out of my wallet along with a $50. I slid them across the table to him.

He took both.

"Look, you said you were a detective, that's why I'm talking to you, but if you're not a cop, then I don't have shit to say to you except last call for you sir, what the fuck'll it be?"

I didn't much like his tone. I decided to correct it.

Red.

Bang.

The metal slammed behind me. Shit. I winced in pain as I tried to open my eyes, the left one swollen near shut. I tasted salty copper taffy congealing on my lips and in my mouth. I pushed myself up, looking around at the waves of black shimmering plastic frothing garbage around me. Damn. I hate when I get my ass kicked. Shooting fires lapped at my ribs as I stood up. That fucking bartender. Engh. At least he had manners. I checked for breaks. Nothing I could feel. I rummaged through my coat until I found the canister, and popped my last couple of vicodin. Hits me in about 20 minutes usually, so I took a few more than I usually did. The alley was grimy, so much trash and sticky shit I hoped was just soda. As I passed the rusted over bile green dumpster, the side door was left ajar; the locking mechanism must have bounced when they slammed it. I reached in, and flailed my hand about. I found the lever, and pulled. The fire alarm deafened me, but as I continued I could hear the screams of people slipping, and glass breaking. "Oops", I thought sardonically, before braying like a hyena as people rushed out the doors. I limped out around to the front of the bar as people spilled out the front door on the other side. I spat ruggedly on the sidewalk, and looked about, getting my bearings. Left. Left was the direction I wanted. Left, left, left right left...hmmm...

I took my notebook from my pocket and checked. I jarringly flipped through it all, trying to make more sense of the sloppy maps, the bad directions, the half jogged theories in there. Since I hadn't gotten much helpful information at the last shithole, I figured I would try the next one on his list.

Black.

Black.

Too much sanity may be madness.
And maddest of all, to see life as it is and not as it should be."
— Miguel de Cervantes Saavedra, *Don Quixote*

*I never remember this part. It comes
and goes in and out of my day, moving
my body
in an effort to keep me alive while my mind vacates for a while.
The black mud moves my body, clumsily at first but slowly
regaining motor skills as I rest, and it wakes up. It comes to save
me from living.
I live, I see,
I hear, I breathe...and I hate.
I need to forget. I don't want to think about these whiny people
and their pathetic, white, middle class America imagined
problems.
I can't stand to look at these
morbidly fat fucks who can't just say no
to the fucking lasagne and
just have a salad once. I am repulsed by the bums who were just
so bored they had to
shoot up or
smoke meth and turned into
some
fucking
Gollum.
I can't stand to look at these boozers, who can't stand their lives
so they just drink up and never make an effort
to improve.*

These fucking loners who can't get out of themselves enough to love someone else, or try to let someone love them,
I mean...there are a shit ton of single people, cheating people...ugly, and hot...statistics indicate that people aren't trying.
Most of all,
I hate that that's who I am.
I can't stand the way I see the world,
I can't stand the way I see myself,
and I can't stand to trust a woman. Not with
my heart,
my soul,
my life.
I try to hold myself to some
standards of excellence, some health and fitness regulation so I can hold my own physically, even drunk. I always look for new music and art, even if most of it is crap these days. I don't think of myself as better, but I try to better myself. In this world, that's insanity. Fighting everything we're supposed to just accept.
I can't.
I can't.

I refuse to.

III

Black.

I needed to step over this smashed, deformed apricot obstructing me. The pit was still covered in placenta and pith. The sidewalk was littered with gum, and tar, and spotted with black, and cracked and caked over with dirt and mud and filth.

Whew. Okay. Just keep focused.

I took in the brilliant whizzing lights, as well as the faint stationary ones I strolled past. Still on Blackstone. I dragged out my notebook. I had left my blue Bic pen in the weakened spine of the page. *The Brig.* Or maybe it's just *Brig*; I wasn't sure, though I'd been there on occasion. I looked up just before walking into a small tree planted on the curb, barely missing it.

It was a nice dive bar, pretty close to my office, so I wanted to stop off there for a few, maybe get some more pills. My back hurt like it had an axe through it. My face wasn't feeling too good either. I had another block to go. I didn't mind the pain so much as I minded the restriction of movement. It's not that I didn't mind the pain, it's that I felt it, red hot. It fuelled a fire in me, added to my hate, my anger, my purpose. I felt it searing through my ribs now, and started laughing. The hurt only fanned out, feeding the engine more, chugging along back to the office now to chug, chug, chug alone. Along. I meant along. Fuck off.

As I passed the liquor store, I pre-emptively dropped in to get some more smokes. The clock behind the counter read 9:21. Pm, I inferred. Money down, carton in hand.

Bang.

The door shut behind me. I couldn't hear the bell this time. I walked to my office door, and tried it. I shook the handle a few times. Locked. Good for you, Jon. I fished for the keys and jangled them about by the lock until something clumsily shifted, and the door swung open with the twitter of squeals. I had left the red on. Good; I lobbed the cigs onto the desk, and slowly shut the door, grabbing the darts from the board on the wall. I went across the room to my chair, and threw myself into it, dropping the darts by the cigs and opening drawers, tossing them for the bottles, which came up after a few frantic search parties. I popped the top of one, and poured a bit of elixar into my rumhole. "Ahhhhh…" I exhaled rather forcefully. Opened the other, and shook out a few oblongs onto the desk.

Bang. Bang. Bang.

I crushed the pills beneath my glass on its coaster, and dusted them into it with my finger, tapping it against the side. I placed the coaster back, and the glass above. I leapt to the bookshelf, slowly knocking over my rotating fan as I went. It hit the floor, writhed a bit, and the metal cage snapped, and the fan was caught. It just sounded like a loud windup toy now, no comfort. I kicked it again, and the motor stopped. It was dead. I went more carefully now to the shelf, and grabbed a bottle of my finest whiskey. I keep nice shit for when I need to recover, or when I need to impress. I was not impressing anyone in this state.

I kicked the ex-fan out of the way and sat back down, threw my notebook on the desk, drowned myself from the tumbler, and smashed the glass against the front window, cracking both. A new web of shadow was cast across me. I looked around, at the holes in the walls, exposing the grains of the woodwork and planks inside the chasms of my walls. Angry clients, often found themselves in a rage. I imagined them doing it, convinced myself and blamed them for doing it, I even billed a guy the first time I did it. After that I realized it was futile to fix it, and I couldn't raise my rates so I just said "Jealous husbands, what are you gonna do?" What was I gonna do?

I sipped on whiskey from the bottle for a while, staring at the web. My life. So well calculated, so well planned and conceived, oh God! WASN'T I GOING TO BE BLOODY SUCCESSFUL!? Ha. The web is as much a construct of mine as a spider's, and no matter how strong, is easily swept away. Unlike spiders, I couldn't spin a new one. Just clung to the strands I had left.

My cigarettes were missing; I could have sworn I just bought them. Ah, here. I tried to grab them with one hand, and managed to grab out with a bruised, gnarled fist and pull the box to my mouth, flipped it open and lipped out a single stick. I summoned a butane Prometheus forth and gasped inward. Hold...and release. Ok, deep breath...and release. Good, another...and release...no more please...but they followed anyway. I got up, still breathing through the tar filled straw, and checked myself. Felt like I had everything. As I locked up again, the roar of an airplane passed overhead. Sounded civilian, though the air force did training at odd hours. They usually made their runs early enough to disturb my peace, but not usually this late in the day. Yeah, probably commercial. I pocketed my keys and headed right.

Black.

I came to the crosswalk here, it was easier to backtrack than wait at the busy light at the main corner. Not cause of the waiting, cause of the lunatics who got a free driver's licence for good behaviour apparently. I was about halfway done with my cigarette, enjoying the cool breath against the hot Fresno air. The health risk was about the same either way. Footsteps slowly clopped up next to me. A moment passed.
"Ooh, child, what happened to you?"
I looked beside me. She was a (presumably) middle aged African-American woman, aged well. She was a large woman, but very proportionate. She was wearing a loose yellow top and designer jeans. She was rooting through her huge purse for something.
"Had a disagreement with someone is all." I forced a small smile.
"Mm-hmm, I heard that one before. What's your name boy?"
"Uh..Jon Ma'am."
"Please...ma'am." She scoffed. She removed some tissues from her handbag, and slowly brought her hand to my face; I moved away just slightly "Hold still now. My name is Nell, baby, Nell Taylor." Her sunflower blouse shifted around her person as she moved toward me. I stood straight again, letting her wipe my face.
"Pleasure to meet you Ms. Nell."
"Ooooh, look at you! A boy with manners; ain't you sweet, honey, who'd wanna beat on you? Now, I got 3 boys, 2 are grown and out the house and the other is growing every day,

haha!" She laughed with gusto, bursting with joy. "I don't know where your mama is, but I'm sure she would do the same for me and mine."

"Oh...She's passed on a while now." I looked at the ground.

"Oh, I'm sorry baby," she was vocally empathetic; her face corroborated. "There are a lot of things we can have in this world but we only ever have one mama." She finished wiping my face. She put the used wipe back in her purse and kept digging.

"Very true. Miss Nell" My face felt cool, refreshed.

"You hungry, sugar? I think I have a granola bar in here, you look like you could eat, and you smell like it too." I looked at her. "Oh, no judging baby, my husband's a drinker, comes home smelling like the full bar. He's a good man though. I sense you're a real good man too." She smiled at me, looked me right in the eyes as I...

"Oh, I wouldn't know about that Ms. Nell." I avoided her eye. Women can always see through us men, especially the ones who've birthed them.

"Well, I think you're a polite young man, and that, in these days is enough to impress."

My lips found themselves moving honestly upward.

"Thank you Miss," I muttered sheepishly. The light turned for me, and foraged onward.

"You take care now you hear, son? I don't want to read 'bout you in the papers tomorrow, or I don't know what I'd do. You stay outta trouble."

I turned, and gave her a grin like we were old friends. "Yes Ma'am." I nodded. I looked deep into her caring brown eyes. She laughed and waved me on my way, bent slightly over over with her hand in her purse and smiling to the ears. It was a delight to be met with such caring. Such real emotions and meaningful human connections were not virtues of the world anymore.

I left the crosswalk halfway through, and walked diagonally across the street, with the rows of glowing sign shouting some obnoxious, unnecessary business in bold, capital fucking letters. I believe there's a lumber emporium somewhere along the way. It's an indoor lumber yard for fuck's sake. A car honked at me from just down the way. I showed him the bird; if I wasn't in his way when he arrived at that point, why did he care if I used a crosswalk or just walked?

I headed a short way into the strip mall before spotting the bar. I walked toward the door. As I entered, I found myself hit with blaring music, always a great introduction. Metallica's *Master of Puppets*. The bar was pretty full, looked like a few bikers, some rockers, a few middle aged rough looking types, most of 'em with dames. Groups of people were huddled around pool tables, squawking away and clamouring about the bar as well. Intimate clans squeezed into booths, tables strewn with empty beer bottles and glasses and crumpled napkins and escaped bar snacks. I stood for a moment, taking in the atmosphere, puffing on my cigarette. A hipster looking woman came over to me.

"Do you mind?" Her voice was whiny and snooty.

"Hm?"

"It's against the law to smoke in bars; me and my boyfriend are just trying to enjoy our night." I looked over at this mousy looking guy with some weird sideburns and a moustache like Snidely Whiplash. These guys must have been some San Francisco yuppies, no one from LA complains about smoke, and no one in Fresno can notice through the air they're breathing already. I gave the woman a look, and tossed my cigarette into an empty beer bottle on the table next to me.

"Thank yoooou!" she sang at me. The fake smile that followed was enough to make a politician vomit, but I held my tongue and kept on task..

I walked over and sat down on the most inviting stool. The bartender was a pleasant looking fellow. He was wearing a white dress shirt, starched. His sleeves were rolled up to his elbows. The black name tag read Kevin I saw as he moved closer.

"Hey, what can I do for you?" He was a cheerful sort of guy. He smiled at me, beaming at me as he wiped down the bar and threw a napkin.

"Uh...I'll have a whiskey...Kevin." I looked at his name tag.

"Alrighty sir, and your name is?" He was still beaming while he worked, almost bouncing. Not with enthusiasm or...just...life. He simply exuded life.

"Jon. Jon Morris." I tried to sound a little more alert.

Bang.

He set the glass down. "Rocks sir?"

"3, please."

"Coming right up."

He pulled the bucket out from under the bar and doled out the ice cubes with the tongs, one at a time.

"So what do you do Jon?" The third cube clinked against the glass.

"I'm a private detective." I said, feeling a bit squirrely suddenly.

"Oh, wow. That must be a really exciting job!" Kevin was genuinely enthusiastic about it; I hated the idea of telling him the truth.

"Yeah, I see some action here and there."

"Oh yeah?"

"No." I said in a fit of integrity, sighing laughs to ease the uneasiness. "Generally the work is boring, most people tak_ the good cases to the police, and a p.i. is rarely good on a cold case. Just part of not being in the business, I suppose. But I've been shot at, got a few stab wounds to my name. Just nothing serious, or conspiratorial."

"I like the old school films."

"What?" I was taken aback by his response.

"Well, Like *Anatomy of a Murder*. It's three hours of detective work, gripping to the last minute. Sometimes it doesn't take a matrix to make a story. Sometimes, in my humble opinion, it just takes a human, a reason, and a process. Doesn't have to be healthy, logical, or anything. But the strangest human process is still human, is still available to anyone who can begin to comprehend the human psyche."

Jesus. This kid did not belong serving me drinks.

"What about someone who only understand the human psyche from the outside, looking in on people?" I figured a rebuttal was deserved, anyone with a head on his shoulders merits a repartee.

"What, like a sociopath?" he laughed. "Most aren't murderers, and very few hang out around here. Hahahahaha!!! I think they take to higher perches." He chuckled loudly away from the glass he was cleaning.

I laughed, "No, not a sociopath. Just an outsider. Someone who's never known enough humanity to understand it, to belonging to it?" I sipped from my glass, slowly. "Say do you go to school here?"

"Fresno State. I think they've done studies on people who have been raised outside of society, or at least society as the majority of humanity exists within it. I imagine it's not unlike being a foreigner."

"You travel a lot?"

His eyes met mine "Whenever I can afford; I love to see all different places, hear new sounds, smell new ground, eat new foods...have you?"

"No." i took a gulp of my drink. "Good luck with State. They have great programs, and I'm not a socialist, just think that money for education should actually be spent on it." I grunted.

"You go there?"

"Dropped out. Great program, amazing professors; no funding." I tapped my glass.

He walked just over to pour me another whiskey, with rocks.

"You want to go back." He read.

"Want doesn't factor in my life. Can I go back? No. Money, bureaucracy, red tape and bullshit. I just gave up on that when I grew up. Did my own thinking, my own research."

He gave short, nervous guffaws. "Well, sir, I have personally found a lot of promise in it. I'm currently studying neuro-psychopharmacology, and the classes are great."

"Jesus. That's a hell of a major; well...at least, I know the very basic idea of it. You like it?" I looked up at him.

"Yes, very much; my professors are very dedicated, in the sciences as well as English. The Philosophy department gets a little bookish and oriented around the newest philosophies, but they just want something to spark any original philosophy again."

"Can't really blame them." I drank some more. "Hey, can I ask you something?"

"Sure" he leaned in.

"Have you seen this guy?" I removed the picture from my pocket.

He looked at it for a minute. "Maybe. I'm not supposed to discuss customers, sir."

"Oh, I understand. He's not in trouble, his sister thinks he's gone missing, I'm just checking up on all of his recorded watering holes." I put the picture back. He continued wiping down the mahogany bar. He was still smiling, but only cordially now.

I tried in again. "Well, look can you tell me where he works, who he hung out with?"

"I don't know where he worked, but... I do know it was cars. Detailing I think. You know, paint jobs, covers, rims, probably knows his way around an engine."

"Was he good at it?" He stopped; looked up for a minute.

"I think so. I never used his place for any work personally, but his friends seemed to like his work, and he seemed to profit from his business. He was always buying rounds."

"What was it called? Do you remember?" I pressed.

"No, I don't think he referred to it by name often, and whichever it is, it's one of many shops in the area around here on Blackstone. I've heard about so much local shit I'd never be able to tell you anything for certain."

"So, what...some kinda hush-hush chop shop?"

"Hey man, I didn't say that, and I never heard anyone else say it either. If I were you, I wouldn't say it here. He has a lot of friends." Kevin looked about at the other patrons.

"Had." I looked at him.

"Had?" He was genuinely surprised.

"Yeah."

"He's dead?" A moment of sorrow flashed across his face, long enough to be true, and short enough to be professional.

"No, like I said...missing. If he had friends, how come they don't wanna find him? How come I can't seem to find them?" I started getting riled.

"I don't know man, they're not here every night, just a few nights a week. Most people bar hop; it might cost in gas, but it's a better way to scope out chicks."

"So is that what he did? Meet chicks?"

"Yeah, he'd buy girls drinks, guys too. I mean a lot of people throw down heavy in bars, it's one of the few hobbies this town offers."

I couldn't help but agree. I felt bad for giving the guy a shit time, he'd been genuine with me, more than I can say for most. I slapped down a 5er on the bar. Gave him a small 2 finger salute, and strolled out.

"Have a good night sir!" He shouted after me.

Black.

Red.

I stare. White. Black. Red.

A bat on acid, screeching about for any sign
of color, for anything recognizable, but the world...it's not right.
Faces are distorted and frightening, people's voices are so...
telling.
It's like seeing everyone in their pettiness, and seeing only three
colors.
Other people can see so much more...
they can see so much good.

I see the guilt, the lies, the darkness, the madness.
I see it.
I see it through red eyes focused on a bleak waste of office
buildings and strip malls and half-farms and pseudo-businesses,
all of them, screaming with color and light, and all of it
distracting from what we need, what we are, who we will
become.

Who will we become?

We all know, every day, who we are, and where we want to be.
When do we get there?
Do we see ourselves as we are?
Do we see ourselves at all?

Do mirrors tell the truth?

IV

I was sitting in *Groggs*, in the back corner by the large front window. Two beers sat in front of me, on individual napkins. One had been half drained. I was waiting for someone else. I always order two beers at the same time if I'm expecting someone; a subconscious habit I picked up (after a few too many dates and meetings got screwed up because of my drinking). I checked my hands. No notes there. I reached for my leather notebook, and found it wasn't in my pocket. Hm. I rarely lost my shit for aforementioned reasons, so I figured I left it back in the office, or in my motel room. Shit, I was pretty sure I needed to pay up for the next week soon...not sure exactly when. I fumbled for my phone; 9:46 pm. As I replaced it, I felt my car keys in my pocket. Shit. I really try not to drive given my nature, but I guess even fucked up I wasn't stupid enough to try and walk this far across the city. I just hoped that I could remember where I had parked.

I sat, drinking, just taking in the people: the men lying about their jobs, the money they make or how much deadweight they can lift. The women pretending they care, and then the very few people, honest enough to be uncomfortable about how much bullshit people feel the need to sling these days to protect their fragile egos, huddled in corners of their own. Without my notebook, I would have to figure this out the old fashioned way. I was sitting with my back to the window, so I figured I must have trusted whoever I was meeting. I only had a couple clients at the time, and there were few of them I wanted to meet in a social bar like this. I figured it must have been Anna. Of course it was. those fucking eyes. Damn it.

Couldn't have stood to get dressed up or anything, could I? This is why I couldn't ever keep a woman.

The people around kept looking at me. I must have looked a little out of place. Maybe I just looked dishevelled. Brooding over a drink. Wearing a dark coat. Sitting alone. Fuck 'em. I got up from the dark wood table and walked past the light stained cedar walls hung with a few well framed posters for beers and bands, and a few pieces of Celtic decor, over to the jukebox, and popped in a few quarters after rooting through my pants pockets. I flipped through the catalogue. It was worn but well tended. K-7. The band struck up.

"People are strange, when you're a stranger..." Jim Morrison crooned.

I returned to my seat, groaning as I sat. My back was killing me. I pulled my wallet out with two fingers and opened it up, took out the Vicodin pills I had put in there and washed it down with my beer. I didn't like taking out a pill bottle in a bar, people tend to frown on it. It's not the 80's anymore. Apparently.

I surveyed the room again. There...there she was, standing there just at the bend in the barroom, looking at me. I didn't know why she didn't just approach when she saw me sitting there; why was she watching me? Her supple hips brought her over to me.

"Hi." she said quietly.

I stood to greet her, "Anna..."

"Have you found anything?", she blurted.

"No, nothing," I saw she looked worried, "...which is usually a good thing, Anna.", I finished. I tried to relieve her. "No one can think of a reason he would be missing, so my assumption is that that's all he is: missing. Have you been in contact with any of his friends tonight? I haven't found his crowd at any of the bars I went to."

She sat down across from me at the table. "I'm not really sure who he hangs out with...I've met a few of them, but I don't know them well enough to have their numbers...what happened to you?" She reached out toward my face, but stopped her hand short.

"Oh, just the job, you know?" I looked away, rubbing a butterfly bandage and a couple of regular flexibles I had across my forehead.

"Was this on my accou...?"

"No." I intervened. "I was working another case earlier. Don't worry; your brother's got my full attention." I lied.

We sat in silence for a moment.

"I'll find him, Anna." I looked into her eyes. There it was again, that green glow of warmth flowing out from them.

        "I miss my mother, Jon." She said, mournfully. She must have missed the comfort and safety of family in a time like this. I wasn't much use at these sorts of things, comfort...

I couldn't remember my mother, much. I didn't know if that was a good thing or bad. I figure whether I loved her or hated her, it must have fucked me up a little either way.

"I'm sorry." I said. I was, but I didn't say it because I was. I said it because I couldn't think of anything else to say. I wasn't used to telling someone something I felt, just what I felt I should say. I wasn't used to talking to someone (without trying to get information out of them, or manipulate them). When someone takes the approach of vulnerable honesty it puts me in an equally exposed position. I don't know how to talk to people like...well...people, anymore.

"Where is she?" I asked, trying to be human.

"Oaxaca".

I had been to Mexico a few times. I loved the country. Well, the parts I've visited. The music, the food, the people, the faith, the celebration of life, age, wisdom...things seemingly lost here. Cabo, San Lucas. That was my haven. White sands, fresh seafood, warm nights, all the cheap alcohol you can drink and rhythmic music to dance to. I don't know why I said none of this aloud.

"Do you visit often?" I had no idea why I was asking such personal and irrelevant questions to the case. I needed another drink.

"No." She looked downtrodden. "It is not possible for me to travel between countries, you know...with..."

"Ah." I thought I understood. If I did, I figured this conversation should end here.

"Excuse me a minute, won't you?"

I got up, bumping into the table with my leg as I did. She laughed. I laughed awkwardly with her, hoping to maybe alleviate the tension that only I appeared to be feeling. I walked outside, and fiddled about in my coat pocket for my cigarettes and lighter. I grabbed my box, and took out one of my pre-rolled joints. It would help me sober up to drive home; alleviate my guilt for arriving in this state. I found them, and struck up the fire. I looked about, breathing lightly through the slightly bent marijuana cigarette. I strolled about for a bit, wandering through the parking lot on bent legs, like Groucho Marx, looking for his car. My face and torso were misshapen in the waxed shimmer reflecting me from the car windows and bending angles of the parked cars. I was drunk and my legs were getting tired of moving. Restaurants lit up the square, couples and groups of friends of all ages walked freely, smiling, laughing, talking. Communicating. All I could think was, if they're talking out loud, they're bullshitting somebody. Ugh. I pinched and inhaled, then threw down the butt of my smoke. I went back inside the bar.

When I returned Anna smiled.

"Sorry." I was uncomfortable.

"It's fine, I was enjoying sitting here listening to the music."

I said nothing, just sat back down across from her and looked into my glass, swishing it around for a few seconds before drinking.

"Would you like to dance?"

"Hmm?" I looked back up at her. I wondered how no one had asked her yet. Or maybe they had. Hmm.

"Dance." She laughed. "You know? Move to the rhythm?"

I was tired, my legs hurt, and I knew that anything I started with this gorgeous fox would end terribly. Or I would end terribly.

"Would you like to dance?" she repeated, as her eyes stared at the table.

No.

Yes, of course.

No. No, you can't.

You are not going to be trapped.

"I would love to." Damn my foul mouth. God she was pretty, and...soulful. We got up, and she took my hand, took me over to the jukebox, slowly leading me there. I felt like everyone was staring, but when I looked around, no one was even looking. They should have been. She was the highlight of the bar, now.

She started to go into her pockets, so I quickly scavenged for a quarter in mine. I handed her two, along with an accidental dime. She smiled, and pushed them slowly into the slot. She took her time, slowly doing a rumba to the rhythm of her anticipation. I watched her movements, enthralled. Like water flowing in a Zen Garden. She pushed a button.

La Flor de Mal: a classic, redone by Tito & Tarantula started to play. I loved that fucking song. I hated spiders, though. We wandered to an open space on the floor, away from other patrons of the bar, and she came in close, and held me there. She rested her head against my chest.

"Your heart is racing." She breathed.

I was nervous, as though somehow, her eavesdropping on my chest would reveal to her every dark secret, every forbidden shame that I kept prisoner there in the dark. I was afraid that she would hear the demons in my soul, growling and scratching their way out, and she would back away. She should. She pulled me to her, and I moved my hands to her hip and shoulder. As we moved more, I slipped my left hand down to her other hip, resting my hands on them just enough, feeling where the curves met. I think it was my favourite part of touching her. When I did, she looked at me as though she knew. Maybe she knew. Was I a pervert? Jesus, fuck no. I mean, kind of; I did like..well, nevermind. But that wasn't it then. I just knew touching her would light up my insides like...weirdly enough like..like I was getting the shit kicked out of me again...the same burning sensation.

I shouldn't be doing this; I shouldn't be this close to her. It's not right. But I couldn't break away, as I smelled her floral hair, her fruit lotion, and the underlying scent that was just her. It was moments like these I wondered if I didn't trust women, or didn't trust myself. I broke away.

"Sorry." I pretended to stumble, hoping she would just think me drunk. I hung my head for a minute. Her eyes bunched up as she laughed; I raised my head again, smiling unconsciously, and we walked back to our seats. I pulled hers out for her. We sat for a minute, sipping our drinks quietly. When we had finished, she looked as though she were having a great time, still rocking to the music, like she didn't want to leave. That was my cue.

Black.

We sat in silence on the drive to her house. I think I made her uncomfortable, but wasn't sure how. Maybe it had been my hasty request to depart. She kept taking sidelong glances at me, each one a staying on my face, as though she were waiting for the opportune moment to say something, or was waiting for me to. I didn't. The rumble of my engine provided the bass, and her long breaths gave a little high end to lighten the score. The streetlights whizzed by like scummy stars, the occasional tree or sign casting strange shadows across our faces, cutting them and masking them. As we turned down a residential street to get to her house, darkness fell. The neighbourhood was quiet.

It always unnerved me how quiet Fresno was. A city...any real city, would have miles of bustling 24 hour business and entertainment and activities. Instead they throw a few main streets near freeway exits, try to make it look presentable, and shut everything (but the 7-11's and bars) down by 10 pm. There were no teenagers out smoking on the street, or riding bikes, or listening to music. There were no bums wandering around looking for recycling to collect from middle class assholes' trash cans. There were no midnight joggers, no joy riders, cruisers, chippys, angsty teens, brooding poets, lost dogs, wandering wayfarers...just..empty darkness, shaded from the moonlight by the trees.

"Thank you." She broke the silence.

"For what? I haven't found anything, I haven't even found any evidence that anything is wrong, and other than people being unforthcoming and forgetful about your brother, in bars no less...I have no reason to be suspicious."

"But you are suspicious, and you are trying to help me. That is more than anyone else in this country has ever attempted to do for me or *mi familia*." She looked at me, eyes wide.

I hadn't realized until this moment that I knew how she felt. I was born in this country, I would die here. Along the way, I hadn't had much in the way of family. I never really found strangers to be kind people. In fact I found humans to be immensely selfish. I had to walk through this world alone, constantly braving the fear of forever being a stranger in a familiar land, yet a land that I had grown up in.

"Oh, this up here, on the right is me." she pointed out her window.

I pulled up in front of her quaint mesa style house. It was dark. I put the car in park, unsure what to say or do, so I left the engine running.

"Nice place." I shifted in my seat.

"Would you like to come in? My roommate should be asleep." she quickly invited, as though she thought I expected...

I looked at her. God she was beautiful. Her jade eyes invaded into mine, making me ashamed that she could see me, and I wished I wasn't there.

"Uh, no. Thanks. I want to try and see if I can get anywhere with your brother's case."

She didn't get out. "Do you always work?"

"Yeah."

"What do you do when you're not working?"

"I sleep." I fibbed.

"Do you?" How the fuck did she know?

"No. I drink." I said, for the first time, feeling ashamed of my extracurricular activities.

"Why do you drink?" She looked at me with pity, and I hated it.

"Look Anna, I really like you, and I know you're trying to help, but I should probably find your brother before you go trying to save me from myself, huh?" I tried to chuckle light-heartedly.

"Oh." She sounded disappointed. "Well, maybe, sometime, we can do this again?"

I knew I wouldn't. I couldn't let her in. "Sure." I lied again. She waited, as though unsure how to end this...who knows what it was? I didn't do anything for a minute, then I looked at her, and smiled, but just politely. I hated that smile, I hated giving it to her, but I couldn't show her a smile, a real symbol of joy. I knew that the minute I let myself feel real joy it would be crushed under the weight of my iniquity. She smiled back, and opened the car door.

"Goodnight Anna." I looked at her longingly, hoping she wouldn't notice. She did.

"Goodnight Jon." She smiled at me, her eyes once again glowing.

Bang.

She closed the door, and walked up to her porch. I watched her go inside, turning to wave to me before shutting her front door behind her. Her porch light went on, the universal signal for thieves to fuck off. I pressed the car lighter, popped a cigarette out of my pack, lit it with the hot coil, and tried to drown my regret, burn it away. I put the car back in gear, pulled away from the curb and headed off toward the office.

Red.

Green.

Life, renewal. Envy.
Envy of innocence, or envy of hope.

Love.

No, no...no. Love is red, red is passion green is...I don't know
green. It paints places and things, but it is a color only.

Now, I see green.
Now I see green looking back
at me in the flashes of my dreams,
the dreams
I convince myself I can't remember, the terrors and failed hopes
I will myself to forget.
The sea, just offshore, is green, and hazel, murky and full of
secrets. The dead that went to the deep were lost, the treasures
too, and all their doings, all their life, summed up for a few hours,
printed in a small box, and forgotten within.
Would I end up, buried
somewhere deep in those inviting wells?
Home,
a home I've never seen, and never will, the green hills
cascading across my sight. Only in photographs for me. This,
this musty, smog infested environment was
home now.
No heart.
No heart to give, to home to have. I cannot live
if all I can do is hate.

I strain, hoping against all of my sanity that I will see green again, but I know...I know it's all just one or the other to me. Truth or Lies. Sane or crazy. Innocent or guilty.
I don't see green, just black, and white, and...
I smelt it. Green. So clean in my lungs...like leaving the city and camping as a boy.

The jade dragon overtook me again, before I was consumed in fire once more...

Red.

Part II

"I know who I am and who I may be, if I choose."
— Miguel de Cervantes Saavedra, *Don Quixote*

Red.

This is all there is. I'm never going to find it...whatever it is.

Waiting...

Waiting...

Waiting for death to come to me.

Maybe it will be sweet, and take me quietly. Maybe the world will end in a bang for me.

As I sit thinking of all the ways I could go, it's hard to decide.

I'm never going to find it...

whoever I am...

The Knight of the Mirrors

Black.

In the opaque world, I suddenly felt warmer...I begrudgingly opened my eyes, looking around, trying to place myself. My cranium felt like I had been hit by Mjölnir from the inside, and shattered outward in a hundred bits. Where was I? Everything looked hazy and bright for a minute: a hospital, a subway, a police station, the drunk tank...was this death? Shit! My eyes widened and I realized where the hell I was, as though I'd never been there before. The bathroom, adjacent to my motel room. It was a good sign, I suppose; not far from work and at the very least cleaner than an alley. Not by much though, thanks to me and the custodial staff's negligence. Though, in their defence, I did leave a "Do Not Disturb" perpetually on my doorknob.

I sat up in the tub, turned on the showerhead, and started draining the pool of water, vomit residue and piss from it. I slowly rose from the white basin, my weak and shaky support beams trying to re-utilize themselves, my feet below trying not to lose their hold. I rinsed the stench of bile from my skin with a little off-brand soap, stepped out, and threw a towel around myself. I stumbled to the mirror and looked; my puffed, bloodshot eyes looked back, glistening. No amount of washing with cold water would rid me of that. I looked down and grabbed the rum bottle, chilling in the ice filled sink, took a swig, and set it down on the fake marble counter.

Bang.

I turned on the faucet. I washed, slowly massaging the cool water on my face, feeling for a moment like life would get better. Then I watched as the blood streaked water slowly melted the ice in the sink until the last one dripped away like my dreams. Lazily, I dabbed my facade with one of the crumpled hand towels draped off the counter. It still smelled. Looked vomit-stained too. Ugh. I looked back at my reflection in the mirror, illuminated by the fluorescent light on the ceiling, and one which hung over the mirror. I looked ...gaunt...haggardly...I looked ill. I could see every pore, every crater of darkness that ran across my face. I could see every hair follicle, growing, slowly shooting out its bristly stalks, red, brown and blond, uneven and unshaven. My face looked flush, even after the washing.

The face stared back at me, blankly...dead. Just like my case.

"What the fuck is this?" I asked.

"*I don't know,*" I replied from the other side of the amalgam portal, "*it looks like you're where you end up every time you can't figure it out to me.*" Suddenly I looked alive...sinister? No, just...hateful.

"Yeah, well...it wouldn't have been this way..." I justified.

"*Yeah? What would have been different? What would you have done differently from all the mistakes you've made? Nothing.*" I was taunting myself.

The worst part of it was that I couldn't come up with any sort of real answer... "Don't start that Golden Age fallacy shit with me, I know I romanticized it, but Christ, when am I gonna catch a break, get to the bottom of something big?"

"*When you get the hell out of this shit hole, of course.*"

"Yeah, so I can go somewhere where the competition's so steep I won't even be able to rake in enough each month for an office? So I won't even be able to grab a motel room for a few nights to shower, and shave, and sleep in a bed? Fuck that. I'm fine here." I lied to him, hoping he wouldn't notice.

"*No you're not. You hate it here.*" My doppleganger insisted.

"No I don't." I slurred back.

"*No...you hate yourself.*"

"SHUT UP!" I shouted, my mouth half shut. I was having trouble moving again.

For a moment, I was silent. I'm not sure what I was thinking, or who was going to speak first. The silence cut through me, to my very core, and in that silence words were spoken by myself, to myself...words I could never un-hear, words I could never truly say were false. I took another consoling drink from the bottle. I was glad there was enough left in this one to last me till I got back to back to my office, however long that would be.

I knew what I was thinking. Hell. This was Hell. Facing myself, my own, naked self, and understanding that I was the monster in the mirror. And worse, I was alone in myself. Utterly alone. I had spent my life, my passion, waiting for something so big that I prayed, deep down, everyone I met was a criminal. I saw every salesman as a con, every woman as a cheater, a gold digger, every punk on the street I imagined selling dope to kids, every cop I saw was dirty. I never let myself trust anyone, 'cause I knew everyone lied.

Love; I swear I never knew what it really felt like. I convinced myself a hundred times over I did, and then...something would just change. I couldn't believe them. They would say I love you, and eventually, I just heard words, noises, spoken over an intercom at a bus terminal, an adult on

Peanuts, hazy and irrelevant to the present. My shadowed self in the mirror remained silent, allowing me to pain myself for a bit.

"What are you doing...?" I whispered.

"*I don't know...*" his voice rose, disdainful of me.

"There's gotta be something..."

"*It's always something with you, never a specific, always an abstract.*"

"Ok...there's got to be a case."

"*You've had cases.*"

"I mean real cases, the real fucking deal not this SHIT!"

"*You lost them.*" The mirror grinned at me.

Red.

Bang.

The wall on the side of him wouldn't heal easily, but neither would my hand. he didn't let up. He never let up.

"*Feel better? You lost them. You were too drunk or too dull to convince anyone you were an effective emissary on their behalf.*"

The face seemed to move closer with each word, just inches away from my face, my hot breath against the steamy residue masking myself from myself, each passing second.

I thought I saw the demon smile, his fangs bared. I wiped down the mirror with one of the filthy dishrags the motel had provided. He seemed to snarl at me, giving me hateful looks. I jumped back, slipping and hitting my elbow and tailbone on the floor.

Bang.

Shit, goddamn it!...

"That hurt." he said, gleefully.

At least I missed the funny bone this time. I pushed myself up, supporting my weight on the edge of the sink. I looked up, and our eyes met again, instantaneously and without remorse. He wasn't letting me go, not this quickly, not this easily. He never did. I stood myself up, dragging my feet slowly toward the countertop, in front of the sink, I looked back at him.

My neck craned at an odd angle, as though unconsciously I believed that from a different view, perhaps I would see myself better. It didn't seem that I could. No matter how I moved my eyes or shifted my gaze, it was like the face in the mirror...it was mine, but still not...as though some part of me had crawled out from within and changed me, changed my looks, just slightly. Was this some kind of Wildean spell? Would I awake to find myself growing more haggard, and my reflection coming to life, coming to steal the youth I had wasted? I drank up again.

Bang.

The bottle hit the counter and fell sideways.

Ha. No. No one would steal my youth, my life; it would be too kind to take away the memories, the blandness that had followed the torrent of my past.

"What are you doing here? Why the fuck did you come here?"

"I...I came here to think, to, to...recuperate, to solve the case to...to figure out what to do?"

"So what are you gonna do?" he said chanting the words at me, childishly.

"I'm..."

"You're gonna lay here in your bilge, getting fucking wasted, and wasting your fucking life away, with another wasted case, another bullshit story! Aren't you? Aren't you, you little fucking shit?"

Red.

"NO!" I screamed as my hand hit the glass, casting a cracked dimple across part of his face. My hand bled, only a little. I couldn't feel it. "Urrrgh!" I picked up the bottle angrily, spilling some on my chest and the floor, and bringing it to my lips violently. I know who I am. I know who I am. I know who I am. I quaffed my gulp of rum. "I know who I am." I said calmly.

"Yes, you do. And you wouldn't be you, if you could help it, would you?" He looked delighted in his distressing me again, tempting me to break the mirror further. I refrained, hoping that maybe, like so many times before, he would help me solve the case, help me figure out what I needed to know. I looked him in the eyes. Those eyes that have always watched me, I saw them...they would glance at me from car windows, from jewelled dessert cases, from shop windows...then they would disappear when I looked directly at them, replaced by my own eyes. But this time, like so many other times I confronted myself, they saw me...and I saw them. I felt my heart rate rise, spike even, immediately. Thunk thunk, thunk thunk, thunk thunk...

Red.

I closed my eyes. I took a deep breath, first from the fan blown motel air, then from the glass bottle in which sat the spices which caused wars and peace, violence and passion...it burned, and I liked it. Still, I sweated it out from my pores, and had to wipe the sweat which had only yet touched my brow and yoke. I opened my peepers and picked up the discoloured towel again, wiping myself down, taking in another deep inhalation of air, hoping to slow my heartbeat. I looked myself in the eye.

"Where is he?"

"Where is who?"

"You know who."

"You?"

"No. Ricardo. Rick, Ricky...you know who."

"I don't know him."

"Still? I mean...we've...we've seen his house, we've heard what Anna has to say...how can we still not know...?"

"Maybe you're looking in the wrong places. Maybe you're looking for the wrong person...in the wrong places." He looked at me, face somber, eyes glassy.

"Who else should I be looking for?"

"Someone else, someone you lost a long time ago."

"Her...?"

He paused before answering, keeping me in suspense. *"No."*

"Who?"

Still, he took his time answering. *"You."*

"I'm right here; you're proof of that."

"But you're not really here, are you? You're not really you, not anymore. Not since you failed, and gave up, and surrendered us to this."

I stared, looking deeply at him, at myself...maybe the mirror was telling me the truth, maybe I was this worn...this mad. No, impossible. I've been a good detective, I've been good at what I do...I get by. I didn't surrender to this, I am who I want to be...I mean..."

"*You mean this is the best you could do, the best you could have been, so you yielded to this...man? You gave up on the idea of the man you wanted to be, and you relinquished yourself to your armchair and a bottle, thinking that if you got drunk enough you would be able to forget. To fucking dismiss it, the voice in the back of your mind telling you're shit, telling you that you can do better, you can be so much more.*" His monologue ended, condescendingly, and cutting to my core.

"Why, why, WHY ARE YOU DOING THIS!?" I screamed at him, punching the wall again, smashing another gaping cavern.

"*Because you tried... to fucking... kill me.*"

I stopped for a minute. He was lying.

I was lying.

"*You...you tried to kill me, from the moment I was born you tried to drown me in a river of liquor, you ass...and all I ever wanted was for you to look at me, to realize I was trying to help...I was trying to save your life. And now...now every time you're too pathetic to figure shit out on your own, every time you have questions of self-doubt you...you dare to come to me, begging, in a drunken fit, for my help. And I do. Because I am who you should have been. I am who you wanted to fucking be! I am you, the better you, the real you...the one you tried to dismiss because you are too fucking weak to do anything about it.*" He growled; each soliloquy of his ended more radically than the last...I couldn't take it.

"No..." I said...backing away from this imitative spectre. "No, you...you're an asshole, you're a hallucination, you're..."

He shut me down. "*I am you...what you wanted to be. I am the frustrated self, the unconscious that you buried here, when this*

city killed your hopes and aspirations...when you let it. You're just an accomplice to your own demise." His calm unnerved me.
No.
No.
No, no, no, no, no....
NO! It can't be fucking true, it can't be. It just....can't. But it is. It's true, he's right...

I imagined myself, taking my blade to him...slitting his throat, watching the man in the mirror spray me in cardinal wave like Shamu and then gurgle and gush...slowly...dropping to the ground as I laughed and coughed up hack from my lungs. I imagined an artistic display of death...one in which my end would be worthy of...I don't know...Shakespeare, Doyle, Poe, Christie...something that would be worthy of those greats, the great admirers of death. The only problem in my mind was...well...my life hadn't been interesting. My demons only tormented me, not others. The real writers, the real mysteries lay in the sickness, the fascinating illness of the brain which sought after numerous victims...but not me. There was nothing interesting about my brain. Nothing to persuade a writer that I, that I could be as twisted as the deformed and brilliant minds of most who had died...That's what it took. Deformity or brilliance. My brain was neither. I was...afflicted. That was all.

I broke down, my face contorted in the mirror, my face a dramatic mask with the mouth turned downward, my eyes watered, and I watered my gut with some more rum to soothe the pain. A few loose drops fell from my eyes, some down my cringing cheeks. It was true. I had given up, I had failed. I wouldn't be this...not anymore. After this case, after all of this...I would change. I would become the man I had always wanted to be.
"I've heard all of this shit before."

Shut up. I would go somewhere quiet...Spain, Danmark, Scotland, Argentina...somewhere I could go fishing everyday. Maybe open up a pub, talk to people, listen to their problems, not trying to solve anything, just trying to lend them an ear that would be...sympathetic. Not pity them, but sympathize, empathize, recognize...

"*No, you won't.*" His voice echoed in my head.

"Fuck off." I spoke calmly now.

Bang.

The mirror cracked some more, a few shards fell off. I supposed I was hoping that if I could twist my own image, maybe I could forget it, maybe I could blame the mirror for the monstrous being it reflected, instead of simply blaming myself for it. I would change. I would become someone better.

Red.

Blood was running off my fingers slowly, onto the counter. The rum bottle was stained with it...red and brown and auburn alike. I wrapped it with one of the filthy dishrags that the motel had provided, one less stained than the others. That would change now. It seeped into it.

Red.

I looked down, and chuckled. My life, running away from me...just like it had always done. I was done with it. I was waiting...

I turned the faucet once more and rid myself of this episode in the waters of the pensive porcelain dish. I ran the water, splashing it haphazardly on my face, then drowning it once more in rum. I lapped up the water running from the sink like a dog or a child, taking in great waves of it. When I had quenched the fire in my gorge, I stood uneasily, and inhaled deeply once again. I did not look to the mirror. It would be no help, not yet. I needed to get back out there and...find answers. I took the cleanest towel, a bath towel lying on the floor by the door which I kept to block the smell of smoke from management, and dried off my head and shoulders. I didn't see my clothes anywhere, so I opened the door, and walked into the darkened room.

Black.

Black.

I am...how did he put it...?...a crow
who doesn't know
how to be a crow. And the others know,
they can tell. Everyone can tell, they look at me, and then
look away, sensing that I am an other.

The humans flock about in their herds, loudly braying and
painting themselves in bright colors and music to attract mates.
The specimens put on their displays, and strange,
antiquated yet modern rituals take place.
I am an observer.
I am the walrus. I am the egg. I am the man.
Fully formed and hardly functional.

Crows.
I could hear them, cawing
in the world. I almost
oozed
back into reality
for a moment, before I thought,
" murder."

Murder.

A murder of crows.

Such an odd sound, as though angry,
mournful and bitter;

caw, caw.

Black

Part III

"All I know is that while I'm asleep, I'm never afraid, and I have no hopes, no struggles, no glories — and bless the man who invented sleep, a cloak over all human thought, food that drives away hunger, water that banishes thirst, fire that heats up cold, chill that moderates passion, and, finally, universal currency with which all things can be bought, weight and balance that brings the shepherd and the king, the fool and the wise, to the same level."
— Miguel de Cervantes Saavedra, *Don Quixote*

Black.

       I can feel it now,
closer.
I feel it every time I leave the office, every time the trickle of
sweat down my neck changes from warm to cool,

I know.

Death is coming.

       I feel its weight on my soul. I feel it's weight in my hand
as I
lift my .378, feeling its
heft, it's
might,
it's power. Death.
I feel it creeping in my poisoned veins, as I lazily place
the barrel against my neck, aiming to release
my spirit upward and outward. 80 proof
not enough, maybe .378 will be.

Not enough proof.
Not enough evidence.
I am not mad.
I am not drunk, I am...
thinking.

I am drunk. Too drunk to drive, but the
walk will give me time...
Time to think?

I think, therefore...I'm not sure.
       I'm not sure it qualifies.

V

Black.

I was sitting in the Red Wave Inn, at the far left side of the dark bar. Shit, another bar you can't smoke in. Per request of the management. The place was busy, but not too crowded. Cool inside; they must have had the A/C on full blast. I had ordered two beers, two taco plates. I checked my pockets, and found my leather notebook. I flipped through to the latest obvious mangling of paper from it, angling it in the red glow of the lights. Scrawled at the bottom of the last page written on was "Lt. Dempsey...Red Wave. 11:30 pm." I took a bite out of my taco. Fucking delicious. I checked my phone again: 11:38. Lieutenant Grant Dempsey was one of the cops in charge of the organized crime unit in Fresno County, he'd bounced around units due to his...I don't know, versatile expertise or something. I wasn't sure if he would show up, and I was hungry, so I took another bite from my food. I sipped my beer; didn't want to get sauced, more, I mean, before asking the guy to help me out...again. Seemed disrespectful. This man had dealt with killers and mobs and terrorist cells before; some p.i. looking for a missing person wasn't going to hit the top of his priorities (even if we were old buddies). The meal was delicious, but I threw plenty of salsa *vérde* from the bottle they put out on the bar anyway.

It wasn't karaoke night, thank god, so I threw some change into the digital jukebox, and poked around the screen.

Ah. *I Am...I Said.* Neil Diamond was a genius. I walked back to my barstool and sat down. I took another few bites of taco, spraying it with the occasional shades of spicy.

Bang.

The gun hit the bar with a loud announcement, and the badge followed suit immediately. He housed them under his trademark brown pork-pie hat.
"You look like shit."
"Thanks." I said, mouthful of food. "I got all gussied up and everything."
Grant plunked down on the stool beside me. "Detective Morris."
"Detective Dempsey."
We clinked our beers together, and he raised a taco in thanks. We drank and ate in silence.

"And I am, lost, and, I, can't, even say why. Leavin' me lonely still..."

"So what the hell did happen to you..." he began.
"Nothing I can tell you about anyway, Grant." Why did my bandages always itch every time someone brought it up?
"Oh come on, it's not like I'm gonna go bust their balls, I just wanna know what stupid shit you did to have your face redecorated."
"Oh , har har." I rolled my eyes as best I could. I finished my taco first, and ordered two more beers, and a shot of sake. It was the only liquor they carried at this bar. Well, I guess it was an Inn, not a bar. I had complained before, but I guess I was the only one. Besides, the food made it worth drinking only beer,

and they had quite a selection of domestic and imported. The local Sequoia brews were the best.

Grant tried to refuse the drinks, but he had stuffed his mouth so full of food that he just sort of choked out a few noises and flailed an arm about. I feigned concern for his sanity with my eyebrows. He just glared and went back to chewing. He swallowed.

"Ass."

"I know." I chuckled breathily.

The bartender brought the beers and cracked them open. Again, we toasted, and sipped leisurely.

Bang.

"So what the hell am I here for, Jon?" He picked up his beer again.

"You mean you didn't just want to grab dinner and drinks?" I raised my shot.

"You're not really my type." He drank slowly, only a reasonable sip.

We laughed heartily, and cheered our glass.

"Honestly though, " he continued spluttering "what can I help with?" He ate.

I drank from my beer. "I have this missing person's case and it's driving me mad. The guy seems like a decent guy, has some rough hook-ups and a shit load of cash at some seedy bars, but not a bad guy, and it seems like his income can be accounted for. He even keeps his own books, old fashioned style. He's a 28 year old Hispanic kid, got his G.E.D. Has a record, but nothing serious from what I've been told, and his sister is the only one who picked him up from county: public drunkenness. He's been looking after his sister since they came here, works at an auto shop near the strip here, I'm gonna check it out tomorrow. Detailing, mechanics, windows. I get the impression he's sort of an artist; people really like his work from what I've heard. Mom is still back in the old country, safe enough from what I understand. No sign of money going there, at least not that I could trace yet. Truth is he seems like a good enough kid. Maybe that's why I want to find him." I gulped down some beer. "Before he gets in with wolves. Wolves like them." I looked around the bar. "Wolves like us." I devoured a spicy bite of chicken. Needed a bit more kick.

"Well do you think any of the more unsavory crowds at the bars he hangs out might have gotten to him?"

I belched loudly into my hand. I motioned apologies, and grabbed the salsa *verdé* again, hoping for another wave of sweat to help cool me off.

"I don't know. I don't get much of a straight answer from some, and most don't pay any attention to anything that doesn't revolve around them."

"Truer words." He nodded, and tipped his bottle neck my way. We toasted again in silence. We sat for a moment, sipping our beers. He glanced about the place. I shot my eyes around, looking at the camera, the jukebox, the guys on the end of the bar who just happened to look at me at the same time.

"Well, how'd you end up with it? I mean sometimes these cases fall through but generally, you know, the police take care of the serious reports, go through all the motions?"

"I don't think this girl trusts the police to find her brother. I don't think she's gone to them or if she has, you know they wouldn't take it yet. I think she has some reason to think that her brother's in danger." I looked over.

"A girl. Of course." He said, rolling his eyes. "And she doesn't trust the police to find him? You think that she thinks...come on man. What...?"

"Or doesn't trust what will happen to him if they do. I'm not sure which."

"Hm. How long has he been missing?" Grant asked through a small mouthful of taco.

"About 2 days." I lied and did the same.

"Sure he's not at a friend's place? Maybe on a road trip?"

No, I thought, taking the last bite of my taco dinner. I'm not. I'm not sure of anything. But I don't think...I don't think that people have been straight with me on this one. This case has one too many liars lined up to be nothing.

"Positive" I lied again. "He's in trouble. Or at least she thinks he is."

"She say why?"

"No, she didn't even say she was really. It's more what she didn't say, what she didn't do." I wiped my mouth with the napkin, then replaced my beer on top of it.

"What didn't she do?" Grant asked, gulping down the last quarter of his beer and wiping his face with the napkin, then replacing it under the empty soldier.

"She didn't call 911. She didn't call the bars. She didn't call his friends and hangouts. She didn't even call me, had to come in person, more secure that way. If her brother was just missing for a day, you call his best friend, you find out who heard from him last and where he was headed. You don't slink into the office of a man licensed to dick around and carry a gun. No, she knew something had happened, and wanted her brother back safe, and not in your custody either." I pointed at Grant.

"Well what sort of illegal shit is he mixed up in?"

"I don't know" I said. "I found some weed at his house..."

"I'll bet you did" Grant said quietly, his eyes rolling upward.

"Shut up. It was good stuff."

"I bet it was." Grant said, under his breath.

"Shut up. That was it. A few beers, no liquor even. He didn't look like he was rolling in cash, and I figure most criminals only stay in whatever business they're in because there's money to be made from it. It's a high risk job being a felonious fellow in this day and age."

"Thanks to improvements in law enforcement."

"Thanks to traffic and atm cams. I think using Big Brother to catch the criminals is cheating Grant..." I chugged my beer a few seconds.

"How is it cheating to stop people breaking the law and endangering people?" He took several huge bites, finishing his taco, and then wiping his mouth with the bar napkin before crumpling it and tossing it down on the wooden bar.

"Well it's just the idea that they had to do all the planning research and legwork to commit the crime themselves, cops already have a team of other people putting together files, combing through evidence, sorting out timelines and alibis, checking everything. Now, on top of that advantage, you throw cameras everywhere and when they catch someone doing something, it's deemed a victory for the police. The criminal has one fair opponent: me. An eye researches his target, finds his habits, his lifestyle. Hell, I know which hand some of the guys I've tailed jerk with. But I mean, I go one on one, *mano a mano*. I take them down at their level."

"Jon, you take down cheating husbands, thieving kids and neighbours, druggies, sluts. What good does any of that do, when all you need is a photo and that's evidence enough for the client? Even with the cameras, a photo doesn't seal a man's fate. I've testified in court to being present for the apprehending of a suspect shortly after footage on the same tape shows him committing an armed robbery. He walked. Jury wasn't convinced it was him, said the sportswear he had on was common and frequent that day, and that the face wasn't clear enough to make out. I walked in on him trying to rob the place, after the silent alarm was triggered, but that...that didn't matter to the jury. They saw a photo, and if the photo couldn't prove it to them there was no way I could. Their eyes were the only things they would trust anymore. But you...oh, hahaha...you throw a photo down and get paid, don't you Jon?" He preached.

He was right, I hated that he had a point.

We sat for a moment, silent. I motioned to the bartender to bring two more, big ones.

"Oh, no..."

"It's on me man." I told him.

"Thanks...What about the mother?" he inquired.

"What about her?" I asked, picking up his last taco and taking a huge munch.

"Couldn't he be sending money back home? It's not uncommon."

Bang.

The drinks came down on the bar.

"Mmm. I don't think so." I said, picking up the stein and taking the first sip of the freshly delivered beverages. "I mean, he would have gotten something for himself. A better television at least."

"Ok, well maybe he doesn't make much." Grant proposed.

"If he was small time, no one would have any reason to make him disappear."

"Hm. Honestly Jon, I'm not sure how much there is to it. I mean, it sounds like there was nothing at his house, he's got no enemies you know, of, no criminal associations you know of, I mean...is he..." he stopped.

"What?" I scratched just under my eye.

He leaned in. "You know, legal."

"I don't know." I stated.

"You don't know?!" His incredulity bothered me.

"Look, if a client comes to me and asks me to do a job, I don't ask for birth certificates or their social security, I ask for proof of cash; show me payment on delivery. Besides, if he was gonna get picked up by immigration it wouldn't be in this state, or this town...not this far southern California. Try Arizona for that number cheif."

"Yeah, that's fair." Grant leaned back in favour of the compromise.

We sat quiet again. He was looking at me.

"What?" I shot, chuckling.

"You know what...", he gave me a concerned look.

"Ah, shit Grant, I'm not being taken in. You think every time a pretty face comes along I get all flustered and can't find my way around a case anymore cause my head's up some chick's ass, well it's not!" I barked. He wasn't entirely incorrect.

"Hey, brother, chill out."

I'm fine. I'm fine. I'm fine.

"I'm fine." I said. "Gimme a minute, I gotta go to the washroom."

"Alright, gramps." He laughed uncomfortably.

I walked through the double doors and through to the men's room. I stood in front of the mirror.

PULL IT TOGETHER!!!

"I'm trying."

Focus.

"What is missing from this case, what am I not seeing?!"

I looked up, into my pale and still bloodied face, studying it, hoping maybe the answer was somewhere there...then I grinned.

"Of course."

Where is the answer to the mystery, every single time?

"The End." I smiled.

I washed off my face with warm water, giving me a dash of color and washing off some more of the red. I jerked down on the lever and released the paper towels from the enclosure, ripping off a long sheet and wiping my hands vigorously. I marched out of the bathroom.

"Dempsey..." I mumbled, "I know where I need to go..." The music was loud, drowned out my thoughts and my voice.

"What? He leaned closer.

"I KNOW WHERE I...need to go. Sorry." I brought it down.

"Where?"

"Caballero Muerto."

"Why there?"

"'Cause that's where he took the most cash, and went the most. I almost forgot about it with all of this getting nowhere tonight."

Black.

Grant was looking at me for a minute, austerely. "It might have just gone...somewhere, Jon...and you shouldn't." His face was grave. I didn't like it; made me feel like a little brother who's about to go into the woods after dark. On top of which, I had no fucking idea what he fucking meant. My face must have shown it.

He started up again. "I mean, don't go to that bar. There's a couple dangerous guys hang in there, into human and drug trafficking; they're the real fucking deal, and they own that side of town. The bars, the clubs, the liquor stores...even the gas stations are run by cousins and shit."

"Who?"

"What?"

"Who." I stabbed at him again.

"Look, Jon..."

"WHOOOOOOOO?!" I yelled.

"Jesus, Jon..." he gave me an incensed sigh. "This guy named Javier Lopez, he's a dealer and a cunnyrunner..."

"A what?!" I laughed, despite myself.

"A cunnyrunner..."

"What the fuck is a cunnyrunner?"

"You know, traffics girls?" Grant was laughing now. "Seriously, though, don't, even, think about it, heard it from a Brit. I know how you get, I know. I've seen you like this before..."

"THIS ISN'T LIKE THAT!" I screamed. People started looking over. I didn't care; I was getting livid now. "It isn't fucking like that." I got up. "What's he look like?"

"Jon. This guy is Big Noise around here..."

"What's he fucking look like, Grant?" I was getting irritated.

"Jon..."

"Grant!"

He sighed, exasperated as I wore him down once again and pulled his phone out of his coat. "One minute." As he scrolled through, I finished his last taco and wiped my mouth coarsely; he showed me a mug shot of a Hispanic fucker, looked like a college linebacker.

"Thanks." I stormed off toward the door just as the barkeep handed the check to Grant.

"Jon!"

He held the bill, looked at it, and started to get up, turning to run after me.

"JON!

I stopped, threw him a wink and a grin, just before he gave me the finger and shook his head, reaching for his wallet. I walked out.

Red.

Red.

It's the color of passion, of madness and rage and love...
everything
that consumed me. The color of blood...
blood: the elixir of life
and death...to give and take, to restore and destroy.

Red is the color that rushes
to my face when enraged or embarrassed, sometimes
lightly kissing my cheeks when I think
of her...after that it simply becomes the bright glow
of the back of my eyelids as my
ears listen to the pump, pump, pump of the red
in my veins, joined by Red Label and redrum lurking
somewhere in my bitter consciousness. On the red slate
of my eyelids
I see the maps of my darkest thoughts, pulsing, pushing the
sludge of my hate through my body, mind and soul...I know
if I open my eyes they will be
scarred into my mind, like lightning
striking when I blink, reminding me...no...

Shut up,
shut up...
shut up,
SHUT UP!
I silence you in the name of the dog.

VI

Water. I was drowning. Ugh. I opened my eyes. Must have driven again. I have no idea how I made it back to my office.

Black.

None of the lights were on. I flung myself back into my armchair, leaving a trail between the puddle of saliva I had left on my desk and my smeared notes and my heavily respirating smoke guster.

The jaundiced glow from the outside lights cut through the blinds and bars, locking me behind a chain link fence of shadow. I pulled the chain on my banker's lamp, letting the red and green comingle, reflecting on the desk, and walked over to the door and the back corner, turning them on as well.

Red.

Better. I blinked, looking about. My office looked same as I had left it. I sat back down behind my desk. I reached down, groping for the bottle. It came up, newspaper stuck to the condensation on the bottom. I whisked it against the desk and it fell to the ground like an albatross flung in the hurricane. Glugging, I looked up at the stucco ceiling, watching as the lights from passing cars occasionally slithered across it. When

I was satisfied, I lowered the bottle, slowly, gently, onto the desk.

Bang.

I stood up. I was very dizzy, but knew just the cure.

I thrust my hand deep into the confines, and removed the packet from my pocket. I unsteadily pulled a couple out, dropping one or two cigarettes, and let them fall to the desk. Successfully holding onto one, I let the pack drop after the others. With a click, flint lit my cigarette, and I took in the world through new lungs. I spit it back out again in a minute with a shallow cough, but another drag always cured that.

The air was so hot. I was starting to burn up, so I took off my coat as I stood up, and tossed it across the back of the left client's chair and loosened my tie. I tried toward the fridge. I tripped over the upturned rug corner, stumbled, and hit my head against my shelf. Goddamn it, that hurt. I dusted off my cigarette and crawled over and scraped opened my fridge for cool air and ice. I slowly took a cube and rubbed it voraciously on the back of my rough neck, followed by my assumedly extra-bruised face, then dropped it in the glass, forcing vodka to chase them in, confining themselves to the tumbler. I snagged another and wiped it across where my head had made contact. I downed the rest of the glass, now given a slight chill. I needed to be good and shitfaced if I'm going to get to the bottom of this. I lay there for a few minutes, tanning in the light of Prospero's black room. I eased against gravity, slowly, with great care for my personal comfort. I had gotten to the point where I hurt so much that any and all pain was both felt and numbed at once.

I stood up, and walked over to the bookcase, placing the tumbler there, next to the stereo, trying to find the right CD. Coltrane, Ella, Led Zeppelin, Billy Joel, Sabbath, Sinatra, Waitts...Sinatra. I pulled the album off of the shelf (dusting off dirt and a few dead bugs) and threw the cracked jewel case open, removing the disk. Usually my ipod did the playing for me, but I do love the old school: vinyl....CD if need be. Never cassette, though. I slid it into place and pressed play, leaning against the shelf for support. The sweet swinging sound of *I Won't Dance* rang in my ears, its beat pumping my heart, keeping me alive.

"I won't dance,
Don't ask me."

But she did. I did. I'm not supposed to feel, am I?

Am I?... Maybe I should let everything go, just sit back, relax, run away...settle down. No. Not for me. I'm too restless, I need to finish my case. But there's always going to be another case, I'll always be waiting for the right one, the right case, the one with intrigue and danger and a real fucking villain.

My office was hot. Too hot. Damn this Fresno heat. I rubbed the back of my neck as I felt a drop of cool sweat slowly start to descend. I wiped it on my pants leg. I walked back over behind my desk and my chair, luckily, caught me. Lopez. Javier Lopez. I remember the name. For some reason, the look Lt. Dempsey had given me when he said it engraved it into my memory.

I carefully used two fingers like chopsticks to retrieve a cigarette from my desk, and lit it. Javier Lopez. Maybe he could end this for me. Maybe I could end this case.

Maybe he could tell me what happened to Ricky, what he had done that he seemed to have disappeared and his *compadres* were laying low. Then again, maybe it would be another dead end. Hopefully not Ricky's. Hopefully not mine. I grabbed the bottle off the desk again, and drank, deeply. I puffed on the cigarette some more. I was feeling...anxious. Drunk, peaceful, but...anxious. I know it contradicts. Humans are contradictory.

I'm...I don't know what I am...I just know who I could have been, if I was strong enough, if I wanted it enough. But I never did. I never wanted anything but the next case, the next bottle. I drank up again, speaking of the devil. The booze, not the case. The case...right...the bar. El Caballero Muerto. I opened my laptop, and looked up the directions after a few spelling corrections. Shit. I'd have to drive again. I set my GPS on my phone, and tried to find a discreet route. That'd have to do, I'd just need to keep driving straight on Blackstone, and Olive, otherwise the darkened off streets would be safe for me, cops never did their beats, not really. I fumbled around my pockets for my keys, and saw them on the desk. I picked them up. I grabbed the darts to follow.

Bang. Bang. Bang.

I hit my target well enough. 12, 5, and 15. Alright, if I could still hit my mark well enough, I suppose I can drive. I decided to leave the red on so I could see well enough to keep from hurting myself when I stumble in later, I want to be able to see my chair. I could already feel it was gonna be one of those nights. I put on my coat, keys in hand, and walked out the door of my office. As I did so, a fly flew in. I would contend with him upon my triumphant return.

Black.

Black.

"Darkness washed over the Dude..."

Coddled in the womb of night, shrouded in cosmic anonymity. Who am I? Does it matter?

There is no response from the darkness. It sits, looking at me expressionless, but I can feel it's judgement.

Mad?
I am anything but
mad. I am the comatose man
who inexplicably walks and talks, but does not
live life. I see,
I see like these...these heathens and Philistines cannot, I see
how we degrade ourselves, how we fall, almost plummet
to our doom, as soon as we make one
corrupted
decision. And these days
everything is corrupted;
nothing is pure. Your sight is blinded by
neon, paparazzi, a 10 minute attention span.
You have lost
the lust
for knowledge, for improvement.
I see beyond. It cripples me with
fear, with disgust. I have to drink to be
able to stand living in
such a world, have to
numb myself
with drugs
before I realize I'm one of these....
cretins.

VII

As I walked through the solid paneled door of *El Caballero Murto*, I was met with the continuation of Motley Crue's power on the radio (though the bar had a better system than my piece of shit car). The atmosphere was thick, but with what...I hadn't yet figured out. I decided to add to it with some Marlboro flavour as I crossed the uneven brown harsh wooden floor. No one took much notice of me, which I took as a good sign. I sat down at a small table close enough to the bar, close enough to the door, and far enough from a dark corner to keep myself from suspicion. I darted my eyes around, taking in everything, everyone. There was a young couple in a booth behind me, paying no mind to what was going on around. Over by the pool tables a gang of Hispanic guys were drinking, playing pool on one and serving drinks on the other. The smoke burned my eyes in this poorly aired place. I just blinked the smoke away.

Bang.

The pool balls clacked together as they broke for the round. A couple cheered, and a few guys jeered. A few douchey looking guys were at the bar, high fiving each other over some shit, I didn't know. An old guy was inexplicably two seats away watching their antics. I wasn't in the mood to take in all this shit, detect every last detail...I was tired of this case. I had no idea what happened, where this fucker is, or why. But I know there were people here who knew about people disappearing. Maybe they knew why. Maybe I would solve this case. Hell, this wasn't even a case anymore, this was just me, trying to get to the bottom of what used to be a case...what turned into some kind of quest. What for, I couldn't ever say.

The bartender came around, and asked me what I wanted. I asked for a whiskey and soda. He stared at me for a minute, stared at my poorly and half-assedly bandaged visage, looking at the red and black that painted its impression. He nodded, and walked off without a word to get it. I laid my $5 on the table for it, just to make sure there'd be no trouble. I wasn't being paranoid, this case has just made me...cautious. More cautious than usual. The bartender brought my order.

Bang.

The glass hit bottom on the thin table. He slipped the money off, and went back behind the bar without a word. I looked around again; nothing interesting at all seemed to be happening, or going to happen, in this bar. Just the pool game.

Bang.

I saw him. He was sitting just out of the light at the very end corner of the bar, by the pay phone perched precariously on the pine wall. Probably used this place as an office.
Javier Lopez.
Great name for an enforcer and a thug, takes the police a day or two to sort through perps before they finally find the right file. He looked about 5'4", but he was sitting down. He was older than the mug shot that Grant had shown me. He looked more, I don't know...experienced. Like a dog who's been kicked one too

many times to trust a shoe. The man was built like a tank, broad and sturdy. He was wearing a black woven polo shirt with jeans, Ray Bans spilling out from the light weave of hair just behind his collar. His beard line was neatly trimmed, thin. It made him look bigger still. He didn't look like he had a gun, but like I said, he was big.

He was watching the tv's, keeping track of some of the scores, sometimes just watching because it was on. I just sat and kept drinking my drink, never lingering too long. My whiskey and soda was getting watered down from the ice melting, so I took this chance to go to the bar to freshen it up. I stood there at the bar for a minute, and the bartender walked over. I slid my glass across to him, and then sat down on the stool in front of me. I fidgeted with the napkins, and munched on the peanuts, then looked over at Javier. He wasn't looking my way, so I kept scanning. When I came by him again, he was looking, so I nodded. Javier nodded back. The barkeep came back with my whiskey and soda.

Bang.

The glass said to the bar. I asked him for a sidecar too, and threw down another 5. I guzzled down the most of the Jack and Coke. He brought the glass and bottle;

Bang.

I downed the shot and half the beer to follow it. Javier hadn't taken his eyes far from me since we had made eye contact, and I figured he knew I was there for him. I also figured he didn't know why; a cop would show a badge, an enemy would show a

gun. I walked over to him, and sat down a few stools away,
around the curve of the bar from him. I looked up at the tv's.
"Anything good on?" I asked. He was silent for a minute.

Bang.

The pool game continued. I smoked.
"If there was, you'd already know *esé*. You're not here to watch
a random game."
"No sir, I'm here for the drinks, and maybe some of the nachos
they serve here, you recommend them?" I wanted to keep him
talking, innocuous, guy talk.
"Do you like nachos?" He asked.
"Love 'em." I drank the other half of my beer down.
"Yeah, do you like tortilla chips with nacho cheese on them?"
I laughed, "Yeah man, that's nachos."
"Do you like them with salsa and sour cream and guacamole
and jalapeños and shit?"
"Yeah."
He looked at me. "Well then unless you think this place can
fuck up chips, cheese, salsa, sour cream and guacamole, I don't
know why you're asking me. Why don't you ask the chef if he
can cook your nachos right? Eh? I'm sure he'd love to hear
about it". He was playful, but threatening at the same time.
"No, I'm sure they'll be fine". I stared at him coolly.
He didn't say anything, just turned back to watching the
basketball game.

Bang.

The bartender came around and gave me another beer.

I sipped it slowly. I looked up at the tv sets around the bar. Nothing I'd put a bet on.

After a minute, Javier turned to me.

"Not hungry?" He asked.

"Hmm?"

"You lose your appetite, man? You wanted to know about the nachos but you didn't ask the bartender." His eyes stayed on my face. A smile played in the right corner of his mouth, just twitching slightly, like he knew me, like he knew that I was here to play a game, and he recognized the opposing jersey from a mile away.

"Oh, I'm not fucked up yet," I lied, "I'll get them after I've had some more to drink."

"Well then why don't we drink?" He asked, smiling.

Bang.

It looked like the billiard game was thinning out. I don't know which team had the upper hand. I looked back at Javier.

He motioned to the bartender 'two', then pointed to where he had moved, one seat away to my left. I was taken aback, but tried not to show it. One minute, he seems to be avoiding me, the next, he wants to have drinks together. Maybe I was gonna get answers the easy way. The bartender brought over two salted shot glasses, a lemon and a bottle of silver tequila. He put an ashtray down as well.

Bang.

Javier swept the glasses toward him, and grabbed the bottle. I extinguished my smoke in the tray that had been provided.

"So what happened to you man?" He cracked the seal, swung off the top and started to pour.

"Hmm?" As I was reaching for the lemon a knife came slamming down.

Bang.

The lemon was halved. Javier stood there, still smiling. He retracted the knife an inch, and with his ring and pinky finger turned the lemon, slicing again and again. He was watching me, not directly, but I could feel his focus.

"Your face", he waved the knife around his features, "who'd you piss off?"

I watched the knife in his hand. He finished cutting, flicked it shut and pocketed it.

"Just a couple guys who didn't like me chatting. You know, I was just being friendly, shooting the shit, and them BAM!" He handed me a shot glass.

"*Salúd.*" He said.

"*Salúd.*" I replied.

We drank. "Ah." I exhaled. He was silent.

Bang.

He smacked his shot glass down on the bar and began to refill. I placed mine down next to it. He filled them both, and slid mine back my way. We clinked shots, nodded, and popped another back. Again, I sighed.

Bang.

He again slapped down the glass and refills. I followed suit.

"So," he said, pouring, "Why does a man who smells of whiskey come to a bar this late to drink tequila."

"I ran out at home and wanted somewhere lively." I half-truthed.

"Oh. You live alone?" Javier drank with me.

Bang.

"Yes." I wiped my mouth on my sleeve.

He was silent.

"If you're out of whiskey, how come you've still got your flask in your coat?" Goddamn this fucker was observant.

"Oh," I tried to keep nonchalant, "sentimental reasons." I patted it.

"To me, sentiment is reserved for *mi familia*, my family, my children, the woman I love. Trinkets of vice have no sentiment, they have to meaning, they give no purpose. They are for those without...purpose."

Javier was right. The closest thing to my heart at the moment was a half full flask of Scottish Whiskey. No parents. No woman. No friends. Hell, I never even had a pet. But the whiskey kept me warm at night, and happier than a man can be sober. I said nothing.

"Order your nachos *hombre*, " Javier ordered.

"What?!" I suddenly snapped, quietly.

"Your nachos. You wanted to see if they were to your *liking.*"

Bang.

The players cheered; it seemed that the pool game was over. One of the guys began to reset the table.

I became suddenly aware of the bartender standing between us, on the other side of the bar. He was looking at me. He wasn't smiling. I looked at him. I was about to speak; he just nodded and walked off to the left into the kitchen, got right to work, as though Javier's confirmation was enough and he needed no verbal contract with me, only direct contact with my blank eyes.

"Why don't we sit down, Mr..." Javier said, walking and motioning me to a table close to the bar, and on the edge of the billiards room, taking the bottle and shot glasses with him. I walked parallel to and behind him diagonally to the square table. He wouldn't get the drop on me, not yet. When I reached the table, I handed him a business card from my pocket across it. He dropped down the glasses and bottle.

Bang.

He laughed. "J.J. Morris. Private Investigator. JJ? What does that stand for?" He kept chuckling, grinning at me.

"Jon James. The Stationary store charged by the letter." I said dryly.

He laughed. I smiled.

I motioned for us to sit, and he nodded and mirrored me.

Bang.

The players broke again.

"Señor Morris, you are not here to drink. Nor are you here to watch the games. You are here for some business with me. While you have yet to state it, you're being unforthcoming about it tells me that whatever it is you want with me, you do not think I will like it. I think you are right." He paused, expectantly, and took a long drink of beer.

I remained silent. The bartender had brought my nachos, and I sat there. Javier motioned for me to try the nachos; I did. They hadn't fucked them up, in fact they were delicious. I picked up a chip, and scooped up the cheese and toppings. Javier never took his eyes off of me as I ate. He poured another round of shots for us.

"Mmm!" I nodded, and pushed the dish toward him, gesturing for him to join me. He waved them away politely. A stray bar fly, however, seemed to have noticed. It buzzed it's way around, and Javier waved it away as well. We drank.

Bang.

I swallowed. *"Gracias."*
"De nada." His eyes never left me.

Bang.

Bang.

Another cheer went up, a good shot at the table I take it.

I continued to munch. He continued to stare.

I looked up at him. "I'm looking for a friend."

"If you were looking for a friend, you would have seen that he is not here."

"I didn't say who I was looking for."

"If you saw him, you would be sitting with him," he pointed, his finger pressed firmly downward at the table we were sharing, "not here with me."

"Well, I suppose I wasn't looking for him here. I was looking for someone who might know where he is here."

"No one here, *amigo*."

"I still haven't told you who I'm looking for."

"Well, *quien es?*"

I rooted around in my coat pocket. He didn't tense up, which I thought was odd. Usually people don't like when I go reaching around in the dark, whether it be my pockets or their secrets. But not Javier. His eyes just stayed on my face.

"Him."

I handed him the photo that I had taken from the house. It was less clean cut than the one which Anna had given me, so I was hoping to elicit a familiar reaction.

He just looked at it.

Bang.

A girl whooped; I assumed another successful play had been made.

"Who is 'him'?" I could stand for him to lose the attitude, but figured for once I would try to be professional..

"Ricky. Ricky Llorena." I kept myself in check.

He looked at it for a minute.

Bang.

Silence. I guess that was the guy that was new, or getting hustled.

"This is recent?" Javier ruffled his brow.

"Yes." I was waiting for him to slip up.

"Hmm. He doesn't have any facial hair or nothing?"

"No, just like you see him there."

"No. I know a couple of Ricky's, but I don't know their last names, and I don't recognize him. Why? You think he's got something to do with me? What do you want him for anyway? He some sort of ex-con?"

"I want to find out what someone else wanted with him. He's missing." I stared at him, matching his eye contact, showing him I was here.

"Hey *amigo*, I don't know anything about no missing persons, I'm just here to watch the games and hang out with my friends."

Bang.

His friends were still playing pool, but one of them looked over. He stopped playing, but kept the pool cue, and slowly headed our way, making half circles, just staring at me. I just nodded to him.

"That's fine man. A friend of mine just heard that some things happen around here, and I wondered if he got involved with something, or..."

"Whoa, back up *cabrón*, what sort of, uh, things...are you hearing about?" Javier was tense all of a sudden, I tried not to show I was even more so. I poured another shot, placed the bottle back on the table.

Bang.

"I don't know, and I'm not here to find out, I'm just here to get this kid home. He's got family missing him; I'm supposed to return him safely."

"And we..." Javier motioned to the crowd now looming, lurking, oozing slowly in my direction with sinister intent, "don't know where he is. We don't know him, *hombre.*"

"A guy spends hundreds and hundreds of bucks here multiple times a week, and you guys, this is your spot? And you don't know him?"

"*Sí, es verdad.* I'm a very busy man, I can't notice every customer at this establishment who comes in and throws down wads of cash. It's a nice bar, it's a classy place. Lots of people come here and spend big bucks, buy drinks for all the *chicas*. I spend a few hundred here a night myself, and except for you, and my friends, as you can see...I keep to myself." He smiled at me.

Red.

I was angry now, and I wasn't sure if I looked it.

"I think you know him. I think he knows you. I think that's why you and your friends here don't want me to find him."

"I think maybe, *mi amigo*, you have had too much to drink. I think maybe it is time for you to go home. I think maybe you would prefer to get your nachos and your snitches from another bar, hmm? Maybe this one isn't to your liking. It can get a little rough sometimes." He looked at me, this time, with an almost menacing expression. His friend with the pool cue moved behind me, just to the right.

"I don't mind a good fight." I smiled.

"I can see." Javier didn't smile back.

I looked into his eyes. He was annoyed. He was done talking. Something happened in that moment; a part of me tried to convince myself I let it, and another tried to prove I was too weak to stop it. I saw him move his left hand under the table. I heard the ripping of tape. Click.

Bang.

Wood splintered. Whiskey ran down my torso, playing in my blood as flask and chest were consummated.

Red

Epilogue

"Until death, it is all life"
— Miguel de Cervantes Saavedra, *Don Quixote*

Bang.
Again, I hear the noise...growing distant now.
Red.
Blood...so much...blood...I just smile, feeling nothing.

Bang.

I'm forced to take a few uneven steps back.
Red.
I start laughing, softly at first and then maniacally. I can't stop myself, something about the cosmos, something I couldn't possibly try to put into words in this moment has become clear, and I can't help but find it ironic, hysterical even. My mouth has twisted from a smile into some grimace of pain and regret, my laughter mimicking my madness...

Bang.

Somewhere behind me, I hear the familiar sound of glass shattering. My vision drops a few feet as I fall to my knees. They're wet, with...
Red.
The floor is red on brown now.

Bang.

I look up wildly at the small crowd surrounding me, faces of hate, of disgust, contorted, jeering faces of men whose lives would mean as little as mine did.

Red.

"There was an iciness, a sinking, a sickening of the heart-".

I look up into the barrel of Javier's gun.

"You shouldn't have come here gringo." He says softly through unmoving teeth, the right corner of his lip turned up in a sneering grin.

I just take a deep breath,

as deep as I can manage anyhow.

I can hear it gurgling, thick red in my lungs.

I breathe out, choking and spitting a little, rattling off a little scat rhythm to end my part with some light percussion before the opus' big finale.

Scat-dat-de-do-dat-da-da-de-do-da-wa...

This is the way the world ends...

Bang.

Black.

Black.

*You ever have a moment when your mind
goes blank?*

*I don't mean like when you're asked
a question when you don't
have an answer, I mean when you are
struck
in a moment with your mind
in the dark, in the void? When the
only reason you know you're even real is because
there is
one
thought that echoes through your head:
No.
Not I think. Descartes proved
nothing. The one thought is
never profound,
always grounded,
solid:
He's dead. She's gone. I'm alone. This is it.
Small, simple, obvious
truths which our
minds, in this lifetime of over-processing and
over-analyzing finally has to
accept something so small, so striking that it hits like a bullet.
My mind is blank. I am grasping for that one thought.
Where is he?*

What will Anna think?
What was the purpose?
Was I close?
Is this it?
What the fuck? I don't know. I don't know. I don't understand,
this can't be all, this can't be all, this can't be all...

This can't be all I was meant for.

Black.

Made in the USA
San Bernardino, CA
09 November 2018